Uglies of the Beauty Salon

Exclusive Special Edition

Ms. BBC

This book is a work of fiction. Names, characters, places and incidents are products of the author's imagination or are used fictitiously. Any resemblance to actual events, locales or persons, living or dead, is entirely coincidental.

Copyright © 2013 by Ms.BBC

ISBN- 9780615897943

Second BBC Promotions paperback edition 2015

10 9 8 7 6 5 4 3 2

Cover design: BBC Promotions

DEDICATION

This book is dedicated to all my girl

CROWN ME

Define Black Queen:

Mahogany, brown sugar, caramel twist complexions giving injections of independence, determination, passionate illustrations of confidence as humanity created me from a rib. Mind, body, and soul. To know who I am, where I come from, and where I'm going, slowly flowing taking each day a step at a time to enjoy their beauty of life you see, for this, Crown me.

The Crown defines strength, power and holiness from God to thy, fear the black man hell they better fear me, being a double minority of this majority they call life, you better think twice and believe in me, I can leap, jump, fly be whatever I want to be, daughter, cook, doctor, sister, nurse, auntie… Go on, Crown me.

Crown me for being black, loving, strong mind, the mother that I am, I may stand on my own but I'm never alone for God is on my side giving me grace and beauty from in to outside. The thickness of my lips, to my fingertips, on the curve of my hips. The way I walk tall and proud as I move about, but surly have no doubt I'll never walk around with my head hanging down, unless I'm receiving my Crown.

This poem is dedicated to all black queens out there. Keep on moving ahead without any fear. If opportunity knocks, go ahead and take it. With God on your side, you'll definitely make it…

Ms.BBC

ACKNOWLEDGMENTS

I would like to express special thanks to various people in my life that have helped me through all the years, to reach this point. To all my friends and family, those who believed in me and those who didn't. To my mother and father for bringing me into this world, my baby mama and mama for taking care of my baby when I was always out reaching for the next "what's next" to build a better life. Thank you for being there to listen. Also, thank you for being the mother I couldn't.

I would also like to thank my home girls, "Simply the best." Thank you for always pushing me harder, wanting me to stay focused, and out of trouble more of understanding my trouble and allowing her to grow before you. Thank you all for being by my side when I was falling, when I thought there was no way but somehow God kept making a way, and you were there when I was lost. Thanks for all the rides and support when you knew I tried to do the right thing, but things just wouldn't go right for me. You all have played a big part in this progress. By reading behind me for years, making me sit at the laptop when I had to make moves just because, and for telling me one day I'm going to be so successful I'm not going to know what to do. Also, thank you for saying stop sitting on all my talent and do something so I can take y'all with me. LOL. To my fav and my angel, I love all of you.

To Mr. Philly Weeden, thanks for all of your advice and inspiration. It helped a lot.

A grateful thanks to Devon Artis for sharing technology with me and for humbling me a bit when I knew it was time, but just didn't want to take it and walking me through self-publishing process.

I would also like to extend my thanks to a very special love that brought me back to life when I was at the point of no return also for letting me be exactly who I needed to be. You opened the very part of me to express my talent that I've been blessed with and have it reach its fullest peak of my life.

Finally, I wish to give great thanks to my baby, Mo-Bunny, for always telling me I'm a great mom when I didn't think I was around enough, for being so much better than me, for me teaching manners, when I should've been teaching them to you, for not judging me when no one understood me. For being your own person and never letting me and no one else change it. You are so beautiful and I've learned so much from you. If you don't know it, you are the best part of my life, the best blessing God could have ever given me. I love you.

To anyone else who feels like they should have been mentioned and wasn't, I honestly give thanks to everyone who has touched a part of my life in some form or fashion. Life experiences have gotten me to this point of my life, so I truly thank you all.

PROLOGUE

BREAKING NEWS

"A young woman has been fatally shot in this alley near Heavenly Hands Beauty Salon. Homicide investigators are on the scene. Witnesses say the woman ran into the alley, looking over her shoulder like she was being chased. She also appeared to be talking on her cell phone.

The next thing I know, BAM, BAM! Shots were being fired and I ducked behind a car. I don't know who did it, but it's sad. I'm tired of this violence on these streets,' said CJ Peters, who works in a nearby coffee shop.

The victim has not yet been identified as authorities are waiting to notify next of kin. We will continue to follow this breaking news story.

This is Tiffany Tarpley reporting for WKYC."

CHAPTER 1

As Dee sat by the window of her storefront salon, Heavenly Hands, she propped her feet up on her booth and took a long sip of the delicious coffee she got next door for free. It was just one of the perks of having her salon next door to one of the most well-known coffee houses in the world. Just then her phone rang. Hearing the Mary J. Blige "Be Without You" ringtone brought an instant smile to her face.

"Hi, baby," she said. "What are you doing up this early?"

"My soul told me my soul mate was awake and that I should call you before you start your day to say I need you," her boyfriend Jeremiah replied in his sexy baritone voice.

Dee laughed innocently. "Awww, baby, that's so sweet. But tell your soul he's too late. He needs to check his watch because I've already started my day."

"Uumm, that laugh's so sexy, so sweet early in morning, making my sheets rise up into a camping tent." Jeremiah tried to rub his cock down, but it was so hard he could barely touch it.

Dee bit down on her bottom lip, imagining the sight. "Stop being nasty, baby. You're making me blush."

"Baby, bring that sexy body over here and let me taste you, and then you can go. I won't try shit else. Scout's honor." Jeremiah put up three fingers as if Dee could see him.

"I can't, Jay. I'm already at the shop and my client will be here soon."

"Damn, Dee, you're always working or busy. Come on, you have to give me something."

Dee looked at herself in the mirror with a sexy glare. "Okay, okay are you still in bed?" she said in a low, sexy voice.

"Yes!" Jay replied, excited to hear the new sexy purr in Dee's voice.

"Uumm, what are you wearing?" Dee asked, as she licked her lips.

"Nothing but my sheets and this hard dick I'm holding just for you," Jeremiah said with a nasty, evil smirk.

"Take off the sheets."

She blew her breath lightly through the phone to let him know she was feeling freaky. "Damn, baby, you look sexy laying there. Close your eyes." Dee rubbed her hands down her thighs.

"Okay, they're closed." Jeremiah pushed down further in his bed to get the right vibe.

Dee whispered in a heavy, breath-filled voice. "Can you feel my body next to yours? Tell me yes!"

"Yes. Yes, baby, I can." Jeremiah loved the nastiness of Dee's imagination.

Dee made kissing sounds as she imagined his rock hard, chiseled body. "Baby, your body's so soft. I love kissing you from your neck to your chest, on this hard flat stomach. Uumm hmm. Say it feels good," Dee whispered to him again.

Jeremiah's toes tingled. "It's not the real thing, but you getting me there."

Dee whined. "Rub your hands down to that cocky. It's hard, isn't it? Rub that long, hard dick. Oooh, baby, let me taste it." She licked her lips.

"Oh shit! Baby, that feels great!" Jay shuddered at the touch of his own hand making love to his own body. He envisioned Dee sucking his sensitive hard dick.

"Rub that dick faster, harder for me. Oooh, baby, you like it? Tell me you like it," Dee demanded.

Jay's toes began to curl. He moaned in pleasure as he groped himself while thinking of Dee's essence and nastiness.

"Tell me when you're cumming, baby. Please. My pussy is so wet for you. Do you feel it? Tell me yes. Tell me yes, damn it!" Dee's voice became more high pitched and sexual like a porn star.

"I'm cumming. Oh, oh shit! Damn, baby." Jay moaned and busted all over his blue 2,500 thread count sheets. "Baby, that's not cool. Damn, you make me want your ass even more," he said, trying to regain himself after releasing a powerful blow. "I need you. I don't want phone sex every time. I'm a grown ass man. I can't keep beating my meat like a teenage boy watching his neighbor through his window."

Dee replied in a baby voice. "I know, baby. How about this? I promise that soon and very soon I will make this up to you. I'll come over and make sweet, sweet love to you in any and every way you would like."

"You better." Jeremiah was serious in his tone.

"Okay, baby. Get up and shower. And when you get to work, think of me allllll day." Dee smiled.

"Yeah, yeah, yeah, you're always on my mind. I'd like if you were on my face."

"All in good time, my dear. All in good time." Dee laughed it off.

Jay became more serious. "Soon. It better be soon."

Just as they ended their conversation Dee's client walked up to the door and peered through the glass to see if someone was in the salon. Dee couldn't stand it because every week her appointment was at the same time. Dee was never late, so she could not fathom why Sally always acted like nobody was at the salon.

Dee swung the door open. "Hey, Sally, how are you today?"

Sally was an older woman who liked to believe she was still young. She had wrinkles all in her face and dark liver spots on her hands. She always smelled of cigarettes. But she wore clothes that teenagers wore, her hairstyles were young styles, and she spoke all the latest slang. Sally knew all the rap songs that were out and she only hung out in 21 and up clubs. The guys she dated were much younger than Dee. Sally acted younger than her kids and they are 21 and 25 years old.

"What's up, Dee? Girl, I thought no one was here. I thought I was gon' have to reschedule."

Dee rolled her eyes. "Have you ever had to reschedule before, Sally?"

"Um, nah, girl. But there's a first time for everything, right?" Sally shot Dee the gun fingers.

Dee rolled her eyes again as she walked Sally back to the shampoo bowl.

"So, what kind of hairstyle do you have for me to work wonders with now?" Dee questioned with a gasp, because Sally was known to bring the craziest styles to her.

Sally laughed hard. "Girl, you know I have one. I saw these hairstyles in the Horizon magazine. I have two colors of hair. I want this short quick weave in a Mohawk with sideburns on both sides."

"Wait a minute! What?" Dee's face went blank. "You lost me. Show me what you talking about."

Sally smacked her lips. "Girl, I know you can make it pop. Hold on. Here they go," she said as she whipped out the magazine. "I'm going turning up tonight so I can get it in."

"Wait, you saying they. Who is they? What you mean?" Dee chuckled and shook her head like she had just come out of a dream.

"See this girl did three hairstyles in both colors. I like all three of them and I want you to put all of them into one." Sally smiled as if there was nothing wrong with what she was saying.

Dee glanced over the hairstyles. "Umm hmm, ok. Come on so I can get you shampooed and under the dryer."

"Hells yes! Come on, baby girl. Get me right." Sally clapped her hands together.

Dee rolled her eyes and continued on to get Sally shampooed.

"Where everybody at?" Sally asked, as she looked around the quiet, empty shop.

"They'll be here soon enough." Dee looked over at the window then continued on with her Sally's hair miracle.

G-mama sat in her car after leaving Peaches' apartment. She loved Peaches very much and was tired of faking the funk about their ongoing side relationship. She was also tired of Peaches acting as if what they had was non-existent.

"*Why do Peaches keep going back home to Big Rob? There's no way he can satisfy her and comfort her like I can*," G-mama thought to herself.

She pouted while sitting in her driver seat and thought about the night they had just spent together. She reminisced about kissing Peaches' body from head to toe and the way Peaches screamed and submitted herself to her. G-mama thought about how Peaches would hold back and lie to her husband and everyone else about their relationship.

"I wish she would just admit I'm the woman for her." G started to get frustrated.

Just as G-mama started the car, her phone began to ring.

"Yep!" she answered.

"Excuse me," Peaches replied with mad attitude.

"Girl, stop tripping. I didn't know it was you. What are you calling me for anyway? I know you can't be missing me already."

"Um, no. I was wondering why the hell you still sitting outside my apartment. Also what time are you getting to work? I don't want us walking in there at the same time and everyone looking at us like we came together."

"What? Wow! Come on, baby. You trippin'. What the fuck would be the problem if we did?" G-mama shouted. "Why you…"

Peaches cut her off while rolling her eyes. "Look! What do think is going on here? I'm not gon' play myself. You need to stop calling me baby before you make a mistake and call me that at the shop. Like I said, what time are you getting to work?"

G hated upsetting Peaches. She tried to make her see they were meant for each other, but how much was she supposed to take?

"I don't know, Peaches. If I pull up before or after you I'll make sure I call to see how long I should wait to come in, okay?" G-mama's voice dropped into a sad tone to make Peaches happy, but G felt like shit.

"Okay! Dang, that's all I ask. Thank you," said Peaches who was suddenly calm and smiling at the control she had over G-mama. "See ya later."

"Yep." G-mama didn't look at the phone to hang it up.

"Cock a doodle doo! Cock a doodle doo! Cock a doodle doo!" The alarm clock went off like a siren in Biggie's ear.

"Okay, okay!" Biggie slammed down on the snooze button. "Ahhhh," she groaned. "I'm awake, here lonely in my bed yet again. Another morning to get up and get ready for school then off to the shop. There has to be more to life than this. Like they say, hard work will pay off, right? Shit, all work and no play is making me a horny toad." Biggie laughed to herself.

She rolled out the bed in her big beautiful ranch style three bedroom house. She walked up to the big bay window she installed in her room herself and opened the blinds wide so the sun could shine in. Biggie did a lot of her own work in her house. It was her work away from school and work to keep herself busy. She finished her bathroom weeks ago. Sometimes she wondered the point in all of it when she had no man and no family to share it with. Well, she had her sisters in the shop, but they all had their own places, all accept G-mama. She loved them all like family, even Peaches who often got on her nerves. It was something about Peaches that just didn't sit well with Biggie.

Biggie got down on her knees in front of her to window to recite her daily prayer. "Dear God, I thank you for giving me the courage to change what I cannot see, to accept the changes of what I can, and the wisdom to understand."

After her prayer she walked into her master bathroom with Jacuzzi tub, a walk-in shower with double shower heads, and a bidet with her glorified chrome-lined toilet. White and light blue tiles covered the walls from corner to corner. A built-in shelf held all the towels, which were rolled and stacked very neatly. Her fragrances, lady products and toilet paper were stacked in a design. She also has light blue and white hand towels with flowers on them hanging from the towel racks and a picture of a baby with a sad face sitting in unrolled tissue hanging on the wall. Her bathroom is her most special place in the house because that's where she gets the pleasure that release her from the stress of her day. She can slide into her tub and masturbate.

Biggie stood there admiring her bathroom for a minute. Then she took a shower and headed out to start her day.

Dee walked outside of her comfortable home wrapped in a long black trench coat with her hair draped down her back. Wearing a pair of black stilettos, she quickly stepped into her 2007 pearl white Armada and started down the street to begin the sweet seduction that would soon blow the mind of one very unsuspecting young lawyer.

When she pulled up in his driveway she smiled at the thought of what was soon to go down. God she loved the element of surprise. Dee walked up to the door and peeked into the window. She saw her soon to be freak walking out of his gym room, sweat rolling down his face and his white-tee.

"Umm," Dee moaned as her clit throbbed at the thoughts she was having. She took her well-manicured finger and pressed the doorbell to hear the ringing of church bells. "It's not Sunday, but someone's going to be blessed today," Dee whispered under her breath as she waited for him to answer the door.

Jeremiah looked at his watch, then at the door, wondering who it could be at this hour. "It's nine a.m."

When he opened the door he saw the sexiest vision a man could have ordered. Dee was standing there with her trench coat wide open, showing only her black lace boy short and bra set and chocolate brown skin. Pure passion was written all over her face.

"Wha... baby, what are you doing?" Jay said, looking in both directions to see if anyone was watching.

"Whatever you want me to be doing, daddy."

She looked over to the next porch to see one of his neighbors staring with his mouth wide open, so she grabbed Jeremiah and dropped her coat on the porch. She kissed her man from his lips, to his chest and to the bottom of the drawstring of his gray jogging pants.

His neighbor was now on his tiptoes trying to see how low Dee was going to go. Jay wanted to stop her, but couldn't because it felt so good. He had been waiting for this moment since they started dating, but he didn't want to move too fast.

Dee was an entrepreneur who was always building her business. Jeremiah thought to himself that if he waited for her, she'd give him the best of her when she was ready. *By God it worked*, he thought to himself. He smiled from his soul at the animal lust in Dee's eyes. She was definitely ready for what he was about to put on her.

Dee was a very sexy and intelligent woman. She carried herself with pure grace and beauty. She had a hell of a personality and a love for life that made him want to get to know her more and more each day.

"Dee, baby, stop come inside. What are you doing?"

Jeremiah started to get nervous as the neighbors glared too intensely.

"I'm doing this." Dee smiled.

She walked up to him and started pulling his shirt up and kissing him on his chest, sucking his pecks, licking his stomach and pulling the string of his jogging pants.

"Ba, ba, baby," he stammered. "Wait, damn. You want some wine or something?" Jeremiah asked, trying not to seem too eager.

But Dee didn't reply. She dropped his white-tee to the floor, pulled down his pants and boxer briefs, pushed him back onto the dining-room table and began to give him the best head he had ever received.

"Damn, shit. Ooh my God. Damn, baby, damn!" Jeremiah cried.

Dee smiled at the fact of making him scream like a bitch while using Gods' name in vain. Jeremiah had a lot to take in, but, she made it happen sucking and licking all the way down to his well hung sac and beyond.

"Um, baby you taste so good. Is it good to you, baby? Huh? Tell me," Dee whispered as she took her lover into her mouth.

Three minutes later Jeremiah exploded in her mouth. He grabbed her hair and screamed out.

"Oh shit. Oooh shit! Fuck, fuck, fuck!" Jeremiah's toes curled and he bit his bottom lip.

That made Dee wet from inside to outside. As Jeremiah's sweet taste rolled down the side of her face, she took her finger and wiped the cum up in one swipe. She licked it all off while looking him in the eyes as if to say, "Do you give up or are you thirsty for more?"

Jay grabbed her by the back of her head and stuck his tongue deep down her throat. He was gentle, but he got his point across. There was a fire going on in her pussy and he had just the right equipment to put it out.

"Cum here." Jay grabbed Dee up off the floor and pulled her up into his arms.

Although she was a big body chick with thick thighs, big hips, and ass and titties to die for, she wore a size thirteen. She carried herself as if she was a size five and no one could tell her different.

Dee has deep brown eyes, the most innocent smile and dimples for days. She never felt uncomfortable in her own skin and kept herself fresh to death all the time. She loved herself from her heart, body, and soul. Dee also loved big boys. Guys that weighed over 250 pounds were the shit to her.

Jeremiah definitely fit that category. Although he worked out daily, at 6'4 and 250 pounds, he was a natural born big boy. He had the sexiest smile. His brown-toned complexion complemented his deep brown eyes. Although he grew up in the hood, he was far from ghetto. In fact, he was a lawyer at one of the biggest law firms in the city. Jeremiah a professional on a daily. He has a very humble side, but he can also get really aggressive when need be, this helps him to recognize the bull-shitters from the rest of them.

Jeremiah carried Dee into his bedroom and laid her on his nigga sized bed. Yeah, you know, not queen or king, but big enough to fit you and fifteen other niggas in it.

Dee was lying there waiting on him to deliver the goods, when he disappeared. Dee thought to herself *what the fuck*?"...Just as she was getting an attitude Jeremiah returned with a bowl of fruit and Cool Whip, and some chocolate pudding.

"I hope you're in for a long night because I got some

shit for that ass."

Dee's eyes widened with glee. She was excited as hell, but still maintained her sexiness. *"He's gon' fuck the shit out of me. Yeahhhh."* She smiled deeply as she thought to herself.

Jeremiah pulled her down to the bottom of his nigga bed, and started kissing her toes, and licking her feet, sucking her ankles, sending her into a sexual horizon, up her leg to her thighs, back and forth from one to the other, Dee couldn't help moaning wanting to scream from just his lips touching her. She knew when the good shit came about she was going to love him.

Jeremiah then slid off her boy short panties and grabbed both her legs and spread her wide-eagle, took one of those large strawberries placed it inside the lips of her soaked pussy and gently began to eat on it right down to her sweet, sweet nectar. Dee couldn't help herself. As soon as his mouth touched her skin she exploded in a way that she had never done before.

He said, "No way. Uh uh. Don't do that. You're not ready yet."

Dee was shaking. "Wha... whatcha talking about?"

Jeremiah took the pudding and Cool Whip and covered her body in it. Then he licked and sucked it all off of her titties, stomach, and ass.

Dee exploded three or four more times and they still hadn't fucked yet. She started to realize he was stealing her thunder and she needed to get it back.

"Hold on, I came over here to blow his mind and he's trying to blow mine. Oh no," she thought to herself.

She reached over to the night stand and grabbed a condom and placed it in her mouth. She flipped him over and slid the condom on using only her mouth. He grabbed the back of the headboard and rolled his eyes in the back of his head. Dee climbed aboard and rode him until the cows came home. She moved her ass slow, then fast, then slow again.

Jeremiah moaned and scratched and moaned some more, calling out to Dee.

"Yes baby," Dee replied.

"DEE!" he screamed.

"Yes baby! Tell me what it is. This shit feels good? You like it? Tell me?" she boasted.

Dee started kissing his ears and neck, knowing it would drive him crazy. Just as the night blew into the window they both exploded in pure ecstasy and fell asleep in each other's arms .They woke up to a morning of round four.....and that was the beginning of a beautiful relationship or was it?

CHAPTER 2

Dee was the owner of one of the largest beauty salons in Cleveland. Although she's a hair stylist, she also has a license as a massotherapist, and she loves everything about it. Every time she walked into her salon, she exhaled at the fact of being her own boss, and having the guts to invest in herself. She had three managing independent contractors who rented booths from her. They were also really good friends of hers.

Her manager "Peaches" was the top hair stylist, a body piercer and the biggest flirt you would ever meet. Peaches was no joke. Often referred to as a "high yellow brick shithouse," Peaches had china eyes, full lips, and a serious attitude. She believed in divide and conquer. If she saw something she wanted she'd go after it with all her might. And after she was done with it, she'd throw it to the side like yesterday's trash. Peaches had a husband and six kids at home whom she truly loved. Her husband was so good to her, but between her career and her family, she had to get her groove on when she needed to.

The first chair stylist was G-mama, a wild woman. You never knew what she was going to do or who even, shit or where. She was definitely a free spirit. But no one judged her for it. G-mama had pretty brown skin. She was thick, but not fat—a sexy diva. She has beady eyes, thick lips and always kept her hair cut short. She was very comfortable in her sexuality: she liked it both ways. Yes, women and men. She'd fuck whomever anywhere, anytime, and anyplace. Although, she was an excellent hair stylist, she didn't have her own place. She rented cars every month and she was always broke. Weirdly enough, she was happy as hell living the way she was living. The girls in the shop loved G-mama and would be there for her when need be.

Last, but not least, was Biggie who was actually the thinnest person in the shop. She stood about 5'9 and weighed 110 pounds. She had a big mouth and a big heart. Biggie was a slim, dark skinned diva. Dee loved her so much cause she reminded her so much of herself. Because just like herself, Biggie got out on her own does whatever it takes to make her dreams come true.

Biggie had long eyelashes, a small button nose, and thin lips. At 30 years old, she was very humble and had only two sexual partners in her life. Biggie was a weave queen. No matter what the style, she could lay it out. She hadn't been doing hair long, but it was her passion. She gave it her all. When she was working on someone's head, it was all about them. Then she could get caught up in the shop drama. And there was always shop drama.

"All right, y'all, it's the beginning of the month so you guys know we're going to be busy. I need y'all to get here on time and get your clients in and out. It's too hot to be sitting up under a lot of people. Okay, G-mama?" Dee glanced at G-mama as she set out the beginning of the month rules.

"Okay, dang! Why you always got to put me on front?" G-mama protested.

"Because you're the one who's late the most!" Dee pointed her finger to the clock.

"Whatever!" G-mama rolled her eyes.

"Wow, wow, wow, Miss Thang! What's with all the 'tude?" Dee looked at G with concern because she was out of character.

"Dee, just leave me alone, okay?" G-mama said in low breath.

"Okay, seems like our girl is having one of her days. She's feeling some type of way. Let's K.I.M —keep it moving," Peaches said with sarcasm in her voice.

"Peaches, did you go to the hair store yet?" Dee moved on to keep the peace.

"Yeah, but they didn't have the relaxer I like. But I did see ya ex-man in there wit his new baby mama." Peaches twisted her lips with gossip finger snapping to follow.

"Whose ex-man?" Dee asked with shock.

"Yo', ex-man, Dee." Peaches chuckled.

"Looking like the perfect little family too." Peaches smiled as she added that tidbit just to be messy.

Dee tried to act unimpressed. "Oh really? Well, I've moved on, so I guess he had to do the same. Dirty rat mouth mofo. All he about to do is cheat on her and get caught like he did with me. Anyway, is that bitch cute?"

"Hell muthafuckin' naw! That bitch look like a real boy. She built funny and she's dirty as fuck. And you know I had to fuck wit her, right?" Peaches smiled hard.

"What you do, crazy ass?" Dee asked, with excitement.

"I walked up to him like hey what's up, Boo? You and Dee get married yet? She gave him this fucked up ass look, like bitch get over here now." Peaches laughed proudly.

Dee laughed. "You're so crazy. She should've kicked your ass."

Peaches rolled her eyes at the thought. "Shit, that bitch would've been having a size eight instead of a baby."

Dee laughed. "You're sick. You know that, right?"

"And you know this, man!" Peaches threw her hand in the air.

"Hey, where's Biggie?" Peaches asked.

"She's not coming in today. She's trying to take some classes down at the YMCA." Dee smiled with pride.

"What kind of classes?"

"Business classes!" Dee answered.

"Really? That's cool. She's always working on K-I-M-ing." Peaches gave a compliment and suddenly remembered more gossip. "Oh yeah, did you hear about J-rock? You know he got arrested last night for killing his sister's man?"

"What!" Dee's eyes widened.

"Yeah, girl. Something about he caught that mofo fucking wit his niece and shit. He beat him to death with his bare hands."

Dee grabbed her chest. "Get the fuck outta here. No way. Ma, you hear this shit?" Dee tried to include G-mama in the conversation to get her mind off whatever she was thinking about.

"Hear what?" G-mama's mind was a million miles away.

"About J-rock killing Boony," Dee played along.

"What? When? Last night?" G-mama snapped back quickly. "Peaches, you sure?"

Peaches darted her eyes. "Hell yeah! I wouldn't say that shit if I knew it wasn't true."

G-mama's eyes moved back and forth. "Why? Wha, what happened?"

Peaches began the story over again. "They said J-rock caught Boony fucking wit his niece."

"What his sister say?" G asked with concern in her voice.

"She's in jail for child endangerment, because the little girl said she told her mother what was going on and her mother called her a liar and told her she better not tell anybody."

"WHAT? What the fuck!" G shouted out.

G-mama had a flashback about her own upbringing. Her friends didn't know why G-mama was so out of it like she was, but she had been molested for many years as a young child. When she asked for help from the people she trusted most, they made her look like a liar, like she was making up stories about her molester. This story about J-rock's niece sent G into a rage in her mind before she knew it. The only person who knew about G-mama's past was Peaches. She knew why G-mama was so upset.

"Damn, y'all stop screaming," Dee warned.

"That bitch need to be put under the jail," Peaches lashed out. She was too hyped to watch her mouth. Plus, she was concerned for G-mama.

"All right, all right, y'all. I got to get my client from under the dryer. Stop all that wild shit." Dee saw the situation getting out of control. She understood the concern for the child, but was unable to see how deep in meant to her co-workers.

"Naw, Dee! You know this shit needs further explaining," G-mama said emotionally.

"Yeah, I know, G-mama. But y'all know how Mrs. Howard is, so let's take a break until I get her ass braided and outta here, okay?" Dee defended with care for G's concern.

"So, Dee you have yet to tell us about your little rendezvous with the attorney." Peaches winked and changed the subject.

Dee giggled like a little girl. "Girl, um, umm, um! All I'm a say is, I love him," she said in her singing voice.

Peaches threw her head back in laughter. "Yo' ass is

sick."

"No, Peaches. Girl, for real. He's so great. At everything too, if you get my drift." Dee licked her lips.

"Oh, I gotcha." Peaches rolled her hips in back of her chair.

"Remember the brother you hooked up wit at the bar that one time?" Dee began.

Peaches looked off into space. "Girl, remember? I dream about him."

"Dee laughed. "Oh shit. Well think about that with rocky road ice cream and homemade chocolate chip cookies."

"Damn. Got damn! So y'all feeling me, huh?" Peaches smiled seductively as she start to drape her client.

"Yeah. Shit, turn the air on." Dee fanned her hands to her face.

"Do you need a smoke or what?" Peaches stopped to see if Dee was gonna explode on herself.

"So, what's up for tonight? Y'all gon' come down to the club? It's ladies night," G-mama chimed in putting the finishing touches on her clients purple and red quick weave.

"Bitch, please. Uh uh, G. You mean ladies night or LADDIES NITE, 'cause if you play me like last time…" Peaches jumped all over G-mama.

G cut her off quickly. "Ho, didn't nobody try to talk to you. I mean, I could have told you it was gay night, but I thought it would be fun to watch you squirm."

"Fuck you, G." Peaches felt embarrassed.

"I know you want me." G licked her lips with seduction.

"Okay, stop the madness. Y'all two gettin' outta line with it. It's like I'm the mama. What the deuce?"

Some of the regular clients laughed at the girls use to them going back and forth in the shop.

Just then the sweet sound of Mary J. started to play on Dee's phone.

"Ooh, it's himmmm."

"It's who?" Peaches teased.

"Him, Peaches, him." Dee laughed.

"Hello?" Dee put on her sexy voice.

"Hey, baby, what's up? Are you busy?" Jeremiah's deep voice boomed through her phone.

"Yes, kind of. I'm at the shop. What about you?" Dee smiled with every word she spoke.

"I just finished in court and I thought you could meet me for lunch."

"Awwwww, baby, that's so sweet, but I'm booked and I won't be free until about eight o'clock tonight after gym class."

"Oh." Jeremiah's tone was laced in disappointment.

Dee felt it. "Don't say oh like that."

"It's just I had a hard morning and I was looking forward to seeing you."

"I'm sorry, baby." Dee pouted her lip.

"It's cool. How about dinner tonight?"

Dee was confused by the sudden brush off. "Okay, but it's gon' be a late dinner. I have to go home and get a shower after the gym."

"Ok, cool. Meet me at BRAVOS at nine o'clock. Is that okay?"

"That's great, baby." Dee smiled big.

"Okay, see you later. Peace," Jeremiah replied in a sexy tone and hung up.

Dee started to do a little dance around the shop.

"Oh boy, you got it bad." Peaches rolled her eyes.

"Forget you, Peaches. You're a hater." Dee threw her hand up.

Peaches laughed hard. "I know you're trippin' now, speaking in your ghetto girl voice."

Dee laughed. "Whatever. You know I sound like you, Peaches."

"Whatever. So what does the attorney have on the menu tonight? And don't tell me it's you."

Dee replied, lifting her eyebrow. "Of course it's not me. I'm dessert!"

"Anyway, just remember no being late tomorrow," Peaches mocked.

"Wha? No. Girl, bye. No you did not go there! I'm able to do what I do and get to work on time. You betta know that." Dee shook her finger at Peaches.

"Excuse me, Ms. Boss Lady. I didn't mean to get outta line." Peaches grabbed her head like she was being beat.

"Whatever, bitch! Just don't let it happen again." Dee laughed and acted as if she was going to slap Peaches again.

"Yes, sir." Peaches laughed and replied in her Celie from The Color Purple voice.

Dee cried in laughter. "Peaches, you crazy as hell, girl."

"Wait, where G-mama go?"

"I think she took the trash out the back," Dee said, realizing she was missing.

"I hope she don't make the mistake of throwing herself away." Peaches snapped her fingers in checkmate.

"See, you know you're wrong for that shit." Dee checked Peaches.

"You play wit trash and it'll get in your eyes. In her case, she just happens to be the trash."

Dee's eyes lit up in shock. "All right now, Peaches! Damn, what the fuck she do to you?"

"Nothing, but don't act like you're not just as tired of her nasty ass." Peaches rolled her eyes.

"No, I'm not. G-mama is who she is." Dee's eyes dropped in disappointment.

Peaches twisted up her lips. "Oh, right. I knew you would take up for her. You always do. Wow!"

"What is that supposed to mean?" Dee's eyes darted at Peaches hard.

"I guess that means I'm your charity case," G-mama said as she walked in.

Dee was embarrassed like she said something wrong. "G-mama, it's not like that. Peaches just be playing..."

G threw her hand up to stop Dee. "No, she ain't playin' nothing. This bitch got beef wit me and always has had beef wit me. The only reason I didn't say anything is, one because of you, and two because the bitch could never say anything to my face."

"I'm not gon' be too many more bitches, so you need to watch that shit." Peaches jumped up from her stool.

"Fuck you, Peach..."

"NO FUCK YOU, G!" Peaches screamed like she had lost her mind.

Dee rushed to stand between them. "Hold on, hold on. Hold up, did I miss something?"

"Nah, Dee, you didn't miss anything. Just know bitches you think are your friends, they're really not. Peace!" G turned with anger in her eyes, grabbed her bag and left the shop. She stomped away like somebody had stolen her bike.

"G! G, come back!" Dee begged.

But it was too late. G jumped into her rental and sped

off.

Dee turned to Peaches. "Do you want to tell me what that shit was about? Peaches, I know you hear me talking to you." Dee questioned Peaches with one hand on her hip and the other one up in the air.

"Dee, just leave it alone." Peaches turned around with sorrow in her eyes.

"Fuck that! You betta tell me something. You know we don't have beef between us in this shop, so either of you tell me what's up or—"

"Or what? What you gon' do, Dee? I'm outta here."

Peaches grabbed her keys and Prada purse and walked out with a diva strut without looking back.

Dee stood there with her mouth gaped open in disbelief.

Later that evening as Dee worked out, she could barely focus. Her thoughts were on her co-workers and how they were at each other's throats. What was she going to do? How was she going to fix it? Why was this going down?

Dee was full of dismay and disgusted. She could hear her instructor calling her name, telling her to "burn more," but she was in too deep. She was going to call Peaches' ass as soon as she got outta the gym. Just then she was brought back with a loud scream in her ear.

"DEE, BURN MORE! GET YOUR LEGS UP! PUSH YOURSELF!" Her instructor was right in her face.

Now Dee was back on track pushing herself through this hardcore cardio class. She finished her hour workout and jumped in her car to rush home and get dressed so she could meet Jeremiah for dinner. As she hopped on the expressway, she yelled out to her phone to call Peaches. Her phone complied. She pressed play on her favorite CD as she waited for Peaches to answer.

"Hello!" Peaches barked with mad attitude.

"Look, are you busy?" Dee gave it right back.

"Yes, I am." Peaches continued her attitude, not affected by Dee's tone at all.

"Well, look, this won't take long. I need to know what went down today between you and G-mama? I'm not gon' let you brush me off like you did earlier. Come on, girl, we're family."

"Damn, Dee." Peaches smacked her lips. "Girl, why do you have to fix everything? Just let it go. We'll be alright. Teeth and tongue fall out, but they can't work without each other. I love you guys, but shit happens. It's cool. Now let it go and get to where your man is, okay?"

"Okay. You sure?" Dee didn't really believe Peaches let it go that easily.

"Girl, bye. See ya." She hung up before Dee could say another word.

In Dee's heart she still didn't feel right about the situation. Something in Peaches' voice sounded fishy. But she was running late to meet her man. As stressed as she was, she needed a little bit of what he was giving.

As she pulled up into the restaurant's parking lot she was still applying her lip gloss, because she rushed out the house after showering she only had time enough to put on her sexiest bra and panties with garter and silk black stockings and black Sophie dress with curve side front split that hugged her thickness in all the right places, with the diamond studded wrap around open toe stilettos. She didn't have time to do all the last-minute touches. She took a deep breath, lay back in her seat and relaxed for what seemed like a lifetime, but was only a few seconds. She looked to her left and saw Jeremiah sitting at a table by the window looking aggravated. She quickly stepped out her truck and rushed inside. Once she reached the table she bent down to kiss him on the cheek, but he moved away.

"You're late!" Jeremiah gave Dee mad attitude.

Everyone was now looking around to see if she was going to pick her face up off the well-shined floor.

"I'm sorry. I got here as soon as I could. It was just—"

"Whatever! I hate waiting. I already had to wait to see you because you blew me off for lunch." Jeremiah shook his head.

"What! I was working—"

"I'm still talking. Don't do that. Don't ever over talk me." Jeremiah demanded more aggressive than he should.

Dee looked around for the cameras. "Is this a joke? Am I being punked? Jeremiah, you are tripping for real. Don't speak to me as if I am a child. I said I was sorry. Since you're in a bad ass mood, I'll catch you another time."

As Dee got up to walk away, Jay grabbed her arm with force. She gave him a you're-hurting-me look and he returned it with a I-don't-give-a-fuck look.

Dee didn't hold back. She screamed, "Get the fuck off me!"

Jeremiah swallowed hard, trying to hold his composure and not make a scene. "Dee, sit down," he demanded through clenched teeth.

Dee glared at him like he was crazy. "Hell naw!" She was ready to gut him like a fish.

Jeremiah looked around at the host who looked

concerned and a restaurant filled with people staring. "Dee, I apologize. Now please take a seat."

"Are you crazy? No way!" Dee threw her purse over her arm and switched her thick ass right up out of there. She jumped in her truck and kept it movin' without looking back.

"That mofo must be crazy. Who the fuck do he think he is? Girl, bye." Dee spoke to herself like she was with one of her girlfriends.

Just then her phone rang.

She looked at her phone and rolled her eyes so hard the tears she was holding back began to fall slowly. Against her better judgment she answered, ready to let him have it.

"Dee, please, baby. I'm sorry. I just had a long day and I couldn't wait to see you." Jeremiah began before Dee could let her words reach her tongue.

"Humph, well you have a very crazy way of showing it." Dee's heart skipped a beat.

Jeremiah hated being called crazy. "I'm not crazy, I just—"

"I know, I know. You had a hard day. Well, so did I. But that don't make me act like a crazy woman, putting my hands on people."

"So did you? Really! You had a bad day?" Jeremiah screamed. "How much of a bad day can you have at a beauty salon!"

Dee took a deep breath and rolled her eyes. "Excuse me. So because I own a beauty salon I can't have stress? Oh, so what're you saying? Your job is better than mine?"

"No that's not what I mean. See, I can't talk to you. You're so inconsiderate, making everything about you."

Jeremiah switched it like Dee was the bad guy.

"Well, let's make it about this: don't call me no fucking more. Peace!" Dee hung up on him and slammed her phone down hard.

Two minutes later her phone vibrated and started to play the sweet sound of Mary J. again. This time she didn't pick up. The phone beeped two times to let her know a message was left. She ignored it and kept driving home, listening to her favorite mixed CD.

Just as she was pulling up in her driveway her phone started to ring again. She really liked this guy, but she refused to deal with a psycho.

"Yes!" Dee reluctantly answered.

"Come on, baby. I really am sorry. Let's talk about this face to face. Please, I need you to be close to me right now." Jeremiah's voice was soft and sexy, making Dee feel weak for him.

Dee sighed. "Jay, don't."

Jeremiah could feel her vulnerability. "Just say yes and I'll be there in a flash."

"I don't know. You really pissed me off tonight and seeing you was the highlight of my day." Dee leaned her head to the side.

"I know, I know. Let me come over and I promise I'll make it up to you." Jeremiah really felt bad.

"Aaaahhhh, okay." She felt like a sucka, but she couldn't resist him. *He did have a bad day*, she thought to herself.

"I'll be there in a second. You won't regret it."

Dee exhaled loudly. "You better hope I don't."

Ten minutes later Jeremiah pulled up in her driveway.

"Damn, he must have been following me home for him to get here so fast," Dee thought.

When he knocked on her door Dee opened it slowly but aggressively to let him know he didn't scare her.

"Damn, our first fight. Awww, baby." Jeremiah said as he stepped inside.

"You can cut out the sweet talk." Dee turned to close the door when all of a sudden the door slammed. Her back was against the door and Jeremiah was in her face.

"Baby, I'm sorry." He looked into her eyes deeply to let her know he was sincere.

"Jay, wha? Why are you looking at me like that?" Dee was a little scared.

"I love you, baby." He kissed her with a passion that sent chills down her spine.

"Baby, baby, ah, ah wait." Dee tried to push him off to regain her breath.

Just as she took a breath, he went down to his knees, lifting up her dress and snatching her panties off with his teeth. Dee couldn't believe it. It didn't hurt her at all. He folded them up and put them in his pocket. He took one of her legs and placed it over his shoulder and began to feast on her pussy as if it was his last meal. Dee reached up at the door although there was nothing there to grab. She was moaning, sweating, and forgetting about everything that happened between them just an hour ago.

Jeremiah took Dee's legs, straddled them over his arms and fucked her up in the air right there in her foyer. She wrapped her hands around the back of his head and allowed him to enter in and out of her bareback, thrusting his dick deeply into her essence.

~~~~~~~~~

Meanwhile, Peaches was sitting in her condo apartment pissed off at the fact that Dee was almost close to finding out her little secret: the fact she fucked G-mama or the other way around. Whatever happened, they both bumped uglies. Just as she was thinking on how she was going to make this thing right so Dee wouldn't be all up in it or make G-mama spill the beans, there was a knock at her door.

"Who the fuck is it?" Peaches knew she hadn't invited anyone over and everyone she knew understood you had to be invited before coming to her apartment.

"It's G."

"What the fuck do you want?" Peaches stopped in her tracks, not ready to see G-mama.

"Open the door, Peaches!"

Peaches opened the door and leaned into it with her arm up the door. "Now the door is open, what do you want?"

"How you gon' play me in front of Dee like that?" G walked in like she lived there.

"How did you know I was here?" Peaches stared at G as she walked by her.

G leaned against the wall and threw up her hands. "'Cause I know you. You're not gon' take no anger home to your family. That's why Rob got you this apartment in the first place, so you can get peace away from home. I wonder how he would feel if he knew you fucked other niggas and bitches all up and through here."

Peaches pierced her eyes at G- mama. "What! Oh, so you think you gon' be the bitch to tell him?"

G-mama grabbed Peaches around the waist, looked her in her eyes and said, "You know I wouldn't do that."

Although Peaches didn't see herself as being a gay woman, she couldn't control the fact that she couldn't resist G-mama. She loved every minute of pleasure G-mama gave to her.

G-mama started kissing Peaches on her neck, right down to her cleavage.

Peaches pushed G-mama away. "G, I'm not gay."

"I know you aren't. Shit, neither am I. Honey, it ain't nothing like a stiff dick up in you sometimes. But other times I want someone to touch me who knows how I want to be touched." G smiled seductively.

G-mama grabbed at Peaches button down dress. A couple of her buttons came undone, which exposed Peaches' full, supple light-skinned breasts. Peaches hated wearing underwear of any kind. She said it made her feel confined. G-mama knew that too and it turned her on. Before Peaches could close her dress back up, G was sucking all over her breasts, kissing and licking them just how Peaches liked it from a man, but better.

Peaches pushed G away again, this time sliding down to the floor, placing both hands over her face.

"Peaches, why are you embarrassed? It's only me and you here. Don't you like the way I make you feel?" G looked at Peaches like she could devour her.

"Yes, I know... but, I do. I can't help it." Peaches' emotions were running wild.

"Just relax. I don't expect anything from you. I just want to make you feel good." G moved in close to Peaches.

G-mama laid Peaches down on the floor and began to give her the greatest pleasure, licking and sucking her pussy like it was a Georgia peach. She fingered her slowly and softly, making her pussy leak juices all over the floor. Then she flipped her over on her stomach and tossed her salad so good she didn't need any dressing. Peaches screamed loudly at the pleasure she was receiving, which only made G more excited. G stuck her tongue deep into Peaches' ass. Peaches dug her nails into the shiny wood floors, squirming and moaning, but that didn't stop G-mama. She then took her thumb and placed it in Peaches' ass. Meanwhile she used her pointer finger and placed it in her pussy and her middle finger on her clit and began to move them all around at the same time.

Peaches rolled her eyes into the back of her head and she came all over the place, screaming.

"Please, G, please don't do that. God please, God please. Please don't tell anyone this shit feel so good."

That made G happy because she never used toys with Peaches so she could feel pleasure without something stiff in her.

Back at Dee's, Jeremiah was still fucking her good. He placed her over the arm of the couch, put one leg up on the arm and pushed his dick firmly inside of her, which made her scream out and gasp for him to relieve it, but he didn't until he was ready.

"Stop!" Dee screamed as she felt the pain thrust up her back.

"Shut up!" Jeremiah said, fucking her with all his might.

As he started thrusting himself in and out of her, giving her pleasure and pain at the same time, he was definitely trying to teach her a lesson for what happened earlier.

"Oooh, shit, baby. Ah! Ohhhhh. Plee, please...please, stoooopppp." Dee begged for mercy.

He kept pounding. "What? Do you want me to really stop? Huh?"

"Yes. No. No! Damn, baby. Shit!" Dee cried.

"Tell me you like it," he demanded, smacking her ass full bare handed.

"Ouch! No." Dee cried some more.

He smacked her ass again. "Tell me you like."

Dee couldn't take it anymore. "I like it. I like it!"

"No, say 'I like it daddy'." Jay began to thrust harder and harder.

"I like it, Daddy. I like it!" Dee began to cry bundles of tears in both pleasure and pain.

"And the next time you keep me waiting I'm gon'—"

Before he could finish his statement Dee cut him off just so it wouldn't get out of hand.

"I won't do it. I promise."

SMACK!

Jay smacked her so hard on the ass his hand stung. "Don't cut daddy off no more, okay?" he said, still thrusting in and out of her. "Okay? You hear me?"

Dee screamed for dear mercy at this fuck session Jeremiah was giving to her. She could hardly catch her breath. The next thing she knew she was cumming all over the place.

Jay grabbed her by her legs. Up in the air she went and he sucked her dry. Dee returned the favor and sucked his dick until he came in her mouth with full force. They both fell over the couch and drifted off into a coma-like sleep.

CHAPTER 3

The next morning the shop was booming more than usual. Clients were rolling through there like it was a grocery store. All the stylists lived up to Dee's request of being on time and getting their clients in and out in record time. Although Dee stayed quiet about the beef between G and Peaches, she was still keeping her eye on them because something was up. She knew that to be true. She just didn't know what it was yet.

Biggie was throwing quick weaves together like nobody's business for most of the day. When she finally got a break, she asked, "So, what did I miss around here last week, y'all?"

"You know what, Biggie? I was here and I missed out on a lot of shit too. Um, Peaches, you care to tell Biggie what we missed out on last week?" Dee asked, her voiced laced with sarcasm.

Peaches laughed out. "Dee, very funny. Big, you know how me and G be going at it, and how Dee be always wanting to fix everything all the time. If you missed anything, it was nothing."

"Well, if y'all didn't leave shit around to be fixed, maybe I wouldn't have to act like the cleanup woman all the time. I mean, damn, you two argue like y'all a couple." Dee tried to remain professional and playful, but was also serious.

Peaches laughed uncomfortably again. "Wow, you hear that G-mama? As if you would have a chance with me."

"What! See, that's the shit I be talking about right there. Why you always trying to upstage on mofos? You know what? People only put other people down when they're trying to cover up their own secrets," G attacked Peaches.

"Secrets? Wow! What kind of secrets do you have, Peaches?" Biggie asked.

Just then Dee's phone began to ring with the familiar Mary J. ringtone. Of course, Dee looked at it and sent the call straight to voicemail.

"Looks like I'm not the only one with a secret." Peaches said.

"First of all, you don't know what you're talking about." Dee said without looking up at her friends.

"Oh, oh so you can be all up in my business, but I can't be up in yours?" Peaches tried to turn the tables on Dee to take focus away from her.

"I didn't say that. It's just…" Dee took a deep breath and her phone began to ring again.

"Why won't you answer it? Isn't that the ring for your new boo?" Peaches pushed deeper.

"Yeah, you're right. I do have something to say. If you guys see him coming, tell him I'm not here and warn me before he enters the door," Dee confessed.

"Is there trouble in paradise?" G asked playfully.

"Yes. Yes, G, there is. I think he's a crazy-ass woman abuser," Dee practically whispered. She was choked up and leaned against her station.

Peaches stopped in her tracks. "Dee, are you serious?"

"Yes, Peaches, I'm serious as a heart attack." Dee's face dropped in sadness.

Biggie ran to the door. "Why are you just saying something now? This mofo could come in here at…"

Just as Biggie was about to finish her statement, Jeremiah came storming in the shop in his Versace blue suit hung nice and neat with his stripe blue tie pulled loose and white hard pressed shirts.

"What! You trying to blow me off and shit? I'm sitting outside calling your phone, watching you click me to voicemail. If you don't want to be bothered, tell me, Dee. Be a woman and let me know. Don't fucking blow me off!" Jeremiah voice was filled with so much rage that the women under the dryers came out and listened with their mouths gaped open.

"You're right, Jay," Dee said with fear in her voice, not knowing what to do because she was still in shock.

"First of all," Biggie stepped up. "This is a place of business. You can't walk in here disrespecting our clients like you own the place. This is a private matter between the two of you and if she doesn't want to answer her phone right now, she doesn't have to. You need to wait until she's ready to speak to you!"

"And who the fuck are you?" Jeremiah looked Biggie up and down.

"Oooh, I'm your worst nightmare if you don't get the fuck up outta here."

"Okay, okay I'm going." He walked up to Dee and grabbed her by the hair. "But I'm taking this bitch with me."

Dee started throwing punches like she was Laila Ali. Biggie jumped on his back and G pulled out a box cutter. They were ready to set it off. Even clients jumped up. Some ran to the side, but the rest were on his ass. He got what he was looking for, or what he wasn't looking for, because they beat his ass. By the time they threw him out, he was cut, burned and bruised up.

"That's okay, bitch! Your posse won't be around all the time," Jeremiah threatened.

"Get the fuck out of here!" G yelled out the door while

throwing his shoe out.

"Dee, are you okay?" One of her clients asked as she rubbed on her back.

"Yes, are you guys okay? Thank you all for helping me. I can't believe him." She started to cry in disappointment. "I'm so glad I wasn't alone. There's no telling what he would have done to me. Thank all of you again."

"Well, not all of us. Isn't that right, Peaches?" Biggie called Peaches out for not helping Dee.

"What? Girl, please." Peaches waved Biggie off like she was crazy. "I don't get in other people's relationship quarrels. Shit, as far as y'all know they'll make up next week and all y'all will be his new enemies," Peaches defended.

"So you're telling me you'd let a mofo beat my ass because you think we'll be together again? So you're saying fuck me; that's my man. If he kills me you're not going to get involved so he won't hate you?" Dee went in on Peaches.

"Yo' man yo' problem is all I'm saying." Peaches popped her lips.

"Damn, Peaches you're so fucked up." G shook her head.

"Fuck you, G. Don't judge me. I'm not gon' get my ass beat for nobody. Fuck that."

"Do you hear yourself?" Biggie stood to the side looking baffled.

"Biggie, look at yourself." Peaches pointed to a mirror. Biggie hair was messed up, she had bruises on her and her shirt was torn off her shoulder.

"It was all y'all and some of y'all still got fucked up." Peaches pointed at everyone.

"So what! Dee is our family. And just like she's been down for us, I'm gon' always be down for her, no matter if I get my ass beat or not," Biggie defended flipping her hair with an I don't care attitude.

Peaches rolled her eyes. "Well, that's you. But like I said, I'm not."

"You know what? It's cool. I don't need y'all to argue the point for me. She feels the way she feels and that's that. Imani, as soon as I come out the restroom I'll get back started on your hair." Dee walked off embarrassed from the episode.

Her client Imani calmly said, "Take your time, Dee."

"Okay, thanks."

In the restroom Dee checked herself in the mirror. She had blood around her mouth and a patch of hair missing. Her shirt was torn and she broke her heel off her shoe. She was more embarrassed than anything. She was pissed off at Jeremiah and at Peaches.

"That bitch! Can you believe her?" she said out loud to herself.

She suddenly recalled the statement G made last week: *The people you think are your friends, really are not.*

"She was talking about that bitch," Dee said aloud. "Okay, okay. That's how it is, huh?"

Dee was suddenly startled by a knock at the door.

"Dee, are you okay in there?" G sounded concerned.

"Yeah, yeah. I'll be out in a minute, G, okay?" Dee responded, as she dabbed wet tissue on her wounds.

"Who are you talking to?" G asked.

"No one, just thinking out loud. I'll be out in a minute." Dee smiled to herself. She didn't realize how loud she had been.

When she walked out the restroom, the salon was

silent. Everyone looked at her with the questioning eyes and genuine concern. She took a deep breath, looked at everyone and smiled.

She clapped her hands together. "I'm okay. Let's turn on some music and get these clients outta here."

"Dee, you can come home with me tonight. I have the guestroom and you don't need to be by yourself," Biggie offered.

"Thanks, Biggie. I didn't really want to go home tonight. I have a feeling he's going to be waiting for me. Even if he isn't, I just really don't want to be there by myself. But can you follow me home so I can get some clothes for a couple of days?" Dee began to tear up.

"Sure, of course." Biggie smiled in sadness for her friend.

They all worked in silence, all in their own thoughts, moving client by client out of their chairs.

Peaches finished up first, grabbed her stuff and left the shop without saying good-bye.

Biggie rolled her eyes. "Can you believe that bitch? She is serious. And you know the only reason she left without saying bye is because she know we going to talk about her grimy ass."

"Peaches don't mean half of the shit she be talking. She was probably caught off guard like we all was." G took up for Peaches.

Biggie jumped out of her seat. "Yes, we all were caught off guard, but we moved our asses, didn't we, G? Why are you always taking up for her? I mean, if I didn't know any better, I would swear y'all two were fucking or something."

G didn't say anything. She just looked at the mirrors and then stared at the floor, not wanting to give eye contact to either one of them.

"Wait. G, oh my God! When Dee said it earlier I was offended for you, but now I see that's why y'all always going at it. That's why you're always mad when she's up in a dude's face. Oh my God! Oh my God, Dee. Can you believe this shit?" Biggie covered her mouth with both hands.

"Biggie, calm down. She must already feel like shit and you're not making it any better. Damn, G. I knew it was something, but I had no idea."

G-mama finally stood up. "What? Whatever! You guys are reading too much into nothing. Ain't nobody…"

"Bullshit!" Biggie cut G-mama off. "G, you know it's true or you would've denied it when I first said it."

"Biggie, calm down." Dee was tired of all the bickering.

"No. No, fuck that, Dee. They put us through arguments and silent treatments every week. We have to walk around on eggshells wondering if they're going to come to blows or not or if we're going to have to find replacements for the both of them." Biggie started pacing. "Damn. That bitch go around judging everybody like she's God's gift to the world and her ass is a dyke."

"All right, Biggie. Watch your fucking mouth. She is not a dyke." G-mama defended Peaches.

"Wooooooo! Take up for your bitch, sweetie," Biggie pushed.

"Bigg, seriously you need to watch your mouth, or…"

"Or what?" Biggie stood up again.

"Guys, guys, look. We will get through this. You're both flipping out on each other and this shit is really about her or not about her. Look, let's not lose our heads on this. I need you guys right now. Please." Dee calmed down the situation.

"You're right, Dee. I'm sorry, G." Biggie hugged G.

"No, it's not anyone's fault." G patted Biggie's back.

Just as the girls left the salon, they hugged each other one last time before retrieving their cars and heading off into different directions.

Biggie following Dee to her house. As they pulled in the driveway they both looked out their windows to see if they saw anything out of the ordinary. When the coast was clear, Dee got out of her truck, walked up to Bigg's car and tapped on the window. Biggie was still looking around and didn't notice Dee coming toward her, so when Dee tapped on the window Biggie screamed.

"Oh, shit, girl! You scared the hell outta me." Biggie was holding her heart. "Where did you come from? I just turned my head for a second."

"Sorry. Well, if I had been him, the both of us would be dead meat. It's cool. I'm just as scared. You want to come in with me or—"

"Girl, bye. I'm going in."

Dee stared at Biggie. "Well, damn, okay. Come on."

The girls walked in the house as if they were leading a horror movie, looking around every corner, ready to battle any moving object. Dee grabbed what she needed and some stuff she wanted for comfort and they dash for Bigg's house.

Biggie walked in the room and turned on the light. "Okay, Dee, this is it, your room for however long you need it. I hope you can be comfortable."

Dee exhaled. "It's beautiful. You know as many times as I've been to your house I've never seen this room. You decorate it yourself?"

Biggie bowed jokingly. "Why yes, yes I did." She

laughed. "You really like it, huh?"

Dee smiled at her friend and got a little serious. "Yes, you are so creative. At least you know you'll always be able to make money doing shit you enjoy. And you took this old house your grandparents left you and rebuilt it into something special. It must be nice to come into an inheritance from rich family members you didn't even know you had and be able to do so many things you've always wanted to do."

"I never looked at it that way before. I always wanted my own business. I just didn't know what I wanted to do. I'm gon' keep that in mind. And with all the money I guess it is helping to get things I want done. I never even think about it. I try my best not to touch the money. I still don't' feel like it's mine, you know? I need to be more grateful. However, right now, I'm gon' take a shower. You can unpack and go raid the refrigerator." Biggie smiled with a peaceful silly look to get a smile out of Dee.

Dee smiled and held her head to the side giving her friend comfort silly smile to let her know she loved her too. "Okay, that sounds great. Hey Biggie, thanks again."

"Girl, please. This is just my way of having some company." She chuckled.

"I guess your cats get bored too 'cause they're all over me." Dee rubbed both cats at the same time.

"I guess. They don't lay on me like that. Get down Scooby and Scrabby," Biggie shooed them.

"It's cool. I need a little loving right now." Dee sat on the bed enjoying the cats' attention.

While Biggie took her shower Dee put her clothes away. She started to cry wondering why this had happened to her. She sat in the window seat, looking out the picture window, watching the rain fall and found herself feeling vulnerable and weak. She hated to feel weak because she was a strong woman and when a woman feels weak it means she let something in her life get the best of her. The more she started to feel the more she wept.

Dee noticed a vision out the window. It looked as if the tree in Biggie's front yard was waving at her. She couldn't tell through her tears and the rain, but she didn't remember a tree when she drove up. And as many times as she had been over to Biggie's house she would have noticed it. She cleared her eyes, wiped her face, and focused her vision.

She saw movement.

"Oh my God! It's him, Big. Biggie, he's here!"

Biggie ran out, falling into walls. "What? Who? Not him!"

"Yes. He must have been at the house and followed us here. I'm so sorry."

"Okay, let's get our minds together and get this mofo for real," Biggie said, while putting her sweat pants on. She went to her closet, pulled out a box filled with all kind of weapons (guns, knives, bullets, brass knuckles, etc.)

Dee's eyes widened. "Umm, Biggie, where did you get all this?"

"You wouldn't believe me if I told you. Now grab a piece and move your ass! Now watch out. Let me at him." Biggie charged toward the door.

Dee quickly grabbed a .38 and ran outside busting caps in the air. Jay jumped in his car and pulled off in fear. Biggie ran up and blew out one of his tires.

"I'm gon' kill both of you Charlie's Angel-acting

bitches!" Jeremiah yelled out the window as he hit the corner.

"Yeah, mofo, and we'll be waiting for your stalking crazy ass!" Biggie screamed to the top of her lungs.

They both returned inside and waited for the police to show, which didn't take long because Biggie lived in a really nice neighborhood and her neighbors were real close. They would not stand for disturbances.

Biggie ran upstairs, put the guns back where they belonged and came back down with a registered pistol. "Ready to play the scared young woman role?" Biggie smiled calmly.

Dee said nothing. She suddenly realized that although she'd known Biggie for a few years, there was a lot she didn't know about her friend.

And Biggie intended to keep it that way.

After the police had come and gone, Dee told Biggie started to clean up and settle themselves they talked and cried together. Dee express to Biggie she was thankful for her help, she hugged her friend tight like a child hugging a teddy bear. She didn't know how to feel about everything that was going on, so she figured she needed to lie down and take it all in, one deep breath at a time.

CHAPTER 4

It's been two weeks since all the drama. Although it was stressful for all the girls, they still had to work and make money to pay their bills. Dee needed to get some relief from her crazy situation and pay her girls back for all of their help and support, so she decided to treat them all to a girl's day.

"Hey, you guys. Why don't we take the day off, call all of our clients, tell them we'll reschedule them for another day and I'll treat you all to a spa day, dinner and a night of nothing but fun?" Dee suggested.

Biggie replied quickly. "Hell yeah! I need some chillax time."

"Okay, anybody else as excited?" Dee smiled

"Sure." G-mama said. "I love anything free."

"What about you, Peaches?" Dee asked.

"No, I'm going to stay here. I have a family at home, in case you guys have forgotten. I can't waste my time kicking it all Willy Nilly!" Peaches snapped.

"Damn, Peaches, you've been really fucked up here lately. What's the problem?" Dee rubbed Peaches shoulders.

"There is no problem," Peaches said with a stank-ass attitude.

"Wooooooo!" Biggie yelled out at Peaches' funk. "What the fuck crawled in your ass and made you stank?"

"You know what, Biggie? Why don't you kiss my ass? It seems to work for Dee!"

"What? Hold on. Wait a minute. What the fuck is that supposed to mean?" Dee put her hand on her hip and glared at Peaches with anger.

"Nothing. Look, excuse me. I just have a lot on my mind right now and I need to be here and make this money, okay?"

"Yeah, whatever! You do that," Biggie said as she walked out the door to gather her composure.

Then the girls cleaned up and started out for relaxation and fun.

When they got to the Touch You in the Right Spot spa they couldn't believe how elegant and free it made them feel. It was one thing to take care of your own clients, but it was something different being the client and being treated like royalty.

The three girls sat in their plush white robes with their feet soaking in pedicure tubs, while drinking some Dom Perignon. The facial masks had hardened so it made it difficult for them to eat the chocolate-covered strawberries, which didn't interest Dee at all because it made her think of him. That is what she was trying to get away from —any thoughts of Jeremiah. . She started sticking her tongue in and out of her mouth because it was all she could do. Her face was as stiff as a board so she couldn't bite into them.

G-mama laughed. "Dee, you're going to get that mask shit all in your mouth."

"G, you should be used to having different shit in your mouth." Biggie took a shot at G-mama.

"Fuck you, Biggie!" G shot back.

"Nooooo thank you. Strictly dickly, bitch." All the girls laughed and joked about that for a couple of minutes. "The one you need to be giving it to is back at the shop. What? You got her on deprive mode?"

G-mama stopped laughing. "What is that supposed to mean?"

Dee felt the mood change. "Come on, y'all. This is our peace away from the shop. Don't bring that drama all up and through here. C'mon, Biggie, why you got to go there?"

"No, it's cool, Dee." G-mama calmed the situation. "Biggie know it's her that want me. That's why she keep putting it on Peaches." G smirked and took another generous sip of her champagne.

"Well, shit, I should want you then," Dee joked. "I wouldn't have to deal with these crazy ass muthafuckers."

They all laughed and moved on to the mud room. After the mud baths and deep tissue massages, the girls now were relaxed and a little tipsy. They went to dinner at one of Dee's favorite restaurants and then danced the night away at G-mama's club. They ordered more wine, sat and watched the people and the enjoyed the DJ play a little reggae music.

Dee let the music take over her body. She threw her hands in the air and moved her hips from side to side. Biggie and G-mama watched as she floated all over the floor. She moved so seductively G had to turn her focus away from Dee in fear of getting turned on. She didn't look at Dee in that way and never wanted to think about her in that way either.

"Can I buy you a drink?" Dee sang with the song, popping her fingers.

The girls were busy pointing and laughing at some of the people who were coming into the club that they were not paying any attention to what was going on with Dee anymore. She moved all over the dance floor feeling free and at peace. She took one step back and suddenly felt the firm body up on her back and the warm mint-scented breath on the nape of her neck.

She instantly froze.

She couldn't breathe anymore.

She was paralyzed inside and out.

Why was he here? How did he find her? Should she scream? Would anyone hear her over the loud music? Does he have a weapon? Was he going to kill her right here in front of everyone? All of those questions went through her head in a matter of seconds.

Just then Biggie was searching through the crowd, trying to locate Dee. "Hold up! What the fuck!"

Biggie investigated. She jumped up and made her way toward the dance floor.

The crowd shifted and what she thought she saw was gone. Dee finally mustered up the courage. She turned around with force to be face to face with her fear, but he was gone. She looked up to find G-mama and Biggie. They saw the fear on her face and immediately knew something was wrong. They left the club and rode home in silence. All of them wondered what the others were thinking, but were too uncomfortable to speak one word.

G-mama broke the silence. "Dee, you don't have to go home. You can go to my aunt's place with me, you too, Biggie."

"Naw, Naw, G. You just trying to get me in your bed," Biggie joked.

They all laughed, but then agreed to stay at G's aunt's house for the night, just to get their thoughts together. G-mama's aunt wasn't home. She was one of those jazzy older women who traveled and shopped all the time. This time she was on a cruise in Jamaica. She traveled there often. G-mama suspected that her aunt had a man there or something because she went to the island at least eight times a year.

G grabbed three wine glasses and a bottle of merlot. She knew that it was Dee's favorite. She carefully poured everyone a glass and said, "Now, what happened?" She took a seat, ready to finally hear the details.

Dee began slowly. "I don't know, actually. I know I was dancing and it seemed like I had forgotten where I was. It felt so good, like I was taking a hot, bubble bath. You feel me?"

"Yeah, yeah. Go on," Biggie said.

"Well, I started to feel watched and it made me a little uneasy. But I'm in a club so of course people are watching me is what I'm thinking. That's when I felt myself back into what felt like a brick wall only with curves and muscles. It paralyzed me. I was so scared I couldn't breathe." Dee's voice started to shake.

"Dee, are you okay?" G-mama asked while rubbing Dee's arm.

"Yes," Dee replied as she rubbed the top of G's hand on her arm. "I'm okay. It's just that I could feel his breath on my neck and his body caressed mine without him touching me really. Without even looking at him, I knew it was him. I knew... Oh God! Why is he..." Dee put both hands up to her face as she broke out into tears.

"Dee, don't cry. It's okay. We won't let him hurt you," Biggie said as she reached in to soothe her friend.

"I'm not crying because of that. Well, I am, but that's not the only reason." Dee took a deep breath.

"Well, what? What's wrong? Dee, what is it? Dee!" Biggie drilled.

"Damn it, Biggie, I'm pregnant." Dee cried out. "I'm pregnant!"

"DAMN!" G and Biggie said at the same time.

"What are you gon' do?" G asked the question they both were thinking, but feared to ask.

Biggie rolled her eyes. "What you mean what she gon' do? She just found out she's pregnant by a maniac. The question should be if she made the appointment to clinic?"

"You not gon' keep the baby?" G sighed.

"Hell no! So this mofo can think he have rights and Dee will have to deal with his ass forever? No fucking way. Dee, I know you're not considering this. Are you?" Biggie stood up in anger to check Dee on her situation.

Dee jumped up and ran to the restroom. She had so much to consider. "Why is this happening to me?" she cried.

G and Biggie felt like shit. This was their girl and she just told them something that had to be scary to find out on her own, and they acted like two big jerks. G grabbed some of her aunt's old albums. She found Billie Holiday lady sings the blues album, cleaned it off and played it at a very middle temple. G started singing along with the song

"Good morning heartache, you ole gloomy side. Good morning heartache thought we said good-bye last night, I tossed and I turned…"

Biggie curled up on the couch, closed her eyes, and listened to her friend's beautiful voice take her into a jazz sadness like no other.

Dee could hear G singing from the bathroom. She loved to hear G sing. It always made her feel like she was in a movie. G loved Billie Holiday and she always knew how to get Dee in a calm mood. Dee came out the restroom and sat next to G-mama and hummed the song in a light peaceful tone, while tears ran down the side of her face.

Biggie got up and found the linen closet where she grabbed some covers and pillows and brought them to the living and started making pallets on the floor.

"We can lay here so if you need to talk we'll be right here for you."

Biggie sat down next to Dee and G-mama. The three ladies sat in silence and cried together until it was dawn.

CHAPTER 5

The next morning while G-mama slept, Biggie went to the clinic with Dee. Although she was not ready for a child, Dee was not sure what she wanted to do, but she wanted to take precautions and speak to someone other than her girls about it.

"Good morning!" said the young redhead nurse to Dee.

"Oh goo, good morning," Dee said nervously. "I'm here to see a doctor about—"

But before Dee could finish the nurse blurted out, "Mrs. Hathaway, oh my goodness. Look at you. You're ready to pop, aren't you?"

"Yes. Yes, I am. Well anyway, I baked you girls some homemade cookies and thought I'd bring them over while they were still warm," Mrs. Hathaway said in a warm southern voice.

Dee stood at the front desk trying to get her words together.

Biggie, standing by her side, was getting aggravated with the nurse. "Um, excuse me, can we please have your attention?"

"Oh, oh my. Please go ahead, honey. I truly apologize. This is my ninth time in here. I know how it goes already." Mrs. Hathaway cleared the air.

"Ninth!" Biggie and Dee said in unison.

"What the fu...?"

"Dee!" Biggie quickly cut her short before she could finish what she was going to say.

After the nurse got Dee checked in, Dee sat and watched in amazement at all the women and how excited they were at being soon-to-be mothers. Most of them wore wedding bands, but the few that didn't still seemed to be okay at being mothers out of wedlock.

She was surprised at how many men were there with their girlfriends and wives. It was amazing. The more she looked everyone over, the deeper in thought she went until she felt like the only one in the room. Her breathing began to fade and the room began to close in on her. If she listened close enough, she swore someone was calling her name. Maybe it was the baby trying to get her attention or maybe it was her mother trying to give her a sign. Either way, she wasn't ready to deal with either one of them.

"Dee, Dee the nurse is calling you!" Biggie yelled, snapping her out of it.

"Come on, sweetie." The nurse rubbed Dee's back as she walked behind her.

Both women walked through the door following the nurse.

Dee turned to Biggie and asked, "Can you wait in the waiting room because I want to speak to the doctor alone?"

Biggie started to refuse, but obliged, not trying to add any more pressure to her friend than she already had.

As the nurse and Dee made their way into the room the doctor started preparing a pregnancy test for Dee to take. Dee was not ready for that. She thought that they would talk first, but she didn't know where to start, so she grabbed the cup, left the room and did her business.

When she returned to the room the doctor was waiting for her. "Seems like you have a lot on your mind?" the doctor said as she placed Dee's pee on the test.

Dee took a deep breath. "Is it that obvious?

"Yes, it's written all over your body." The doctor

never looked up from the test.

"Well, I'm not sure what I'm going to do."

"Well, this test is positive, so you better think fast. Have you spoken with the father? Do you know who he is?"

Dee eyes darkened. "What! Hell yes I know who he is. What kind of question is that? Oh, because I'm a black woman you think I'm just out here fucking anything with a dick?"

The doctor waved her hand. "Please calm down. I apologize. I didn't mean it that way. I was asking if you may have been raped or attacked because you have bruises and you seem so worried."

Dee exhaled in embarrassment. "Oh, ooh, I'm so sorry. I thought you were implying... Please forgive me. I didn't mean to be so out of control."

"It's okay and if you weren't paying close attention I'm black too," The doctor smirked with attitude.

They both laughed.

During the next thirty-five minutes Dee revealed her feelings about the baby and the father. The doctor gave her really great attention and made her feel confident to make her own decision.

After they were done they walked into the waiting area. Biggie jumped up from her almost sleeping position and so did the cookie lady with nine children.

"Oooohhh, sweetie, we were so worried about you." Mrs. Hathaway gave a warm smile.

Dee looked around as if someone had to be standing behind her.

Mrs. Hathaway responded. "I'm speaking to you honey, the look on your face has definitely changed from when you went in. Well whatever decision you make, remember it's yours to make. Don't let anyone take that away from you. Yes, children are a blessing, but so is peace of mind."

Biggie smiled as she walked over to grab Dee's hand because although she at first thought Mrs. Hathaway was a nutty cookie herself, the advice she had just given Dee was the best advice she could ever hear from someone with children.

Dee and her friend walked to the car with more peace in their hearts than what they came in with. Dee had made up her mind as to what she wanted to do. She planned to pray about her decision and let God do his work. Who could argue with that?

CHAPTER 6

"You nasty stankin' ass, dykin' ass bitch!" Rob yelled at Peaches with fury.

"Baby, please, you're tripping. Wha, what are you talking about?" Peaches begged.

"Come on, Peaches, do you think I'm stupid? Do you honestly think I'd get you that apartment and not take precautions? I kind of had a feeling you were cheating on me, but I kept shaking that shit off. But to find out you're not only fucking around, you're fucking with a bitch! A bitch, Peaches!" Rob balled his fist and punched her in the face.

POW!

"Oooh my God! I can't believe you just hit me!" Peaches cried out.

"Get used to it." Rob lost it.

BAM! SMACK!

"Aaaaaahhhhhhhh," Peaches moaned. Her entire body was in pain. "Somebody help me. He crazy! He crazy!" she screamed and tried to run out the door.

Peaches' husband grabbed her by the back of the head and kneed her in the face and threw her down to the floor. Peaches started to crawl away, but Rob wasn't finished yet.

Peaches cried through a bloody mouth. "BA, BABY, please stop. You have it all wrong. I love you."

"Bitch, please! Do you think that shit is gon' work on me? I have it all on tape, baby!" Rob said out of breath.

At that moment Peaches knew she was busted. She was painfully aware that her husband finally knew her big secret. What could she say? As blood dripped from her mouth and body she managed to get to her knees and try to beg for his forgiveness, and he let her. He pulled his dick out of his pants and told her to suck it as they watched the tape of G-mama fucking the shit out of her. Blood was running out of her nose and into her mouth, but she opened her mouth and did what her husband asked of her. Just as she began giving him pleasure, he kicked her in the stomach.

"You nasty bitch! Why would you do this to us? Why would you hurt our family like this?"

"I'm sorry," was all that she could manage to whisper.

Although she would cheat on him, she truly loved her husband and didn't want him to leave her. She would do anything to keep him from putting her out. Unfortunately that's exactly what he did. . He had her things packed up and he threw her out on her ass! And forbid her to go to the apartment he was paying for also.

The next day Peaches went back to work after a long night of sleeping in her car because she needed to make money to pay for her a place to go. When she pulled up she saw that Dee and Biggie were already there and didn't want to explain what had happened. What she didn't know was that she had more explaining to do than what happened between her and her husband. They already wanted to know what was going on between her and G-mama.

"Oh my God, Peaches! What happened to you?" Dee screamed out.

Peaches mumbled. "Um, I... I was mugged!" She cried dry tears because she had no more left in her tear ducts after all that went down with her husband. Besides, it hurt too much to cry with her busted lip and swollen jaw.

"What!" Biggie yelled, looking out the door to see if

the mugger followed Peaches to the shop. She realized the coast was clear and ran to Peaches side.

"Damn Peaches, what did Rob say? I know he went crazy when he saw you!" Biggie continued.

Peaches took a deep breath to get her lie together. "Actually, Biggie, I didn't tell him. I just didn't want him to get all crazy and get his homies all together, looking for someone they may not be able to find. You know how Rob is. He'll shake down every nigga in the world to find out who it was. So you guys can't say nothing either."

"Why not? You have to go home to this man. How are you going to explain that busted eye and swollen lip?" Biggie was aggravated with Peaches' decision.

"I don't know, Biggie!" Peaches screamed out and fell to her knees crying. "I don't know!"

Dee went down to the floor with her, wrapped her arms around Peaches and held her as tight as she could without causing her any pain.

"It's okay, sweetie. Sshh. It's okay. You can come stay at my house until you're ready to tell him. We can just say we're having a saving-Dee-from-the-maniac-baby-daddy sleep over," Dee joked to comfort her friend and put a smile to her beat up face.

Peaches looked up at Dee and said, "Baby daddy?" She wiped her face from the few tears that came out in between dry blood peelings falling down. "Dee, you're having a baby?"

"Yes, I guess I am." Dee rubbed her belly at the fact she had just made a decision without thinking.

Peaches could not say her words clearly because her jaw and lips are so banged up. "What! Awwwww. Dee, did you tell him yet? So are we happy, sad or what?"

"Sshh, we have nine months to talk about this. Let's

get the first aid kit and clean you up. Do you want to go the hospital?"

"No, I'm fine," Peaches quickly replied. "I don't want to have to explain what happened and they might want me to call the police and inform my husband and I'm not ready to talk about it with them or anybody else."

"O.M.G! Why not? This mofo out there beating up on women and robbing them and God knows what else and you don't want to stop him?" Biggie said with attitude, not feeling the b.s. Peaches was giving.

"Biggs, calm down." Dee was surprise at Biggie's reaction.

"No, Dee. Fuck that! There's something she's not telling us and I know it." Biggie pointed her finger at Peaches.

"Big, I'm serious. She's been through enough. Sometimes you just need time to calm down. This is what I know, not what I've heard, okay?"

Biggie looked at Dee in sympathy, feeling Dee knows all too well what it feels like to have unprovoked bruises. She went to get the first-aid kit and helped Dee clean Peaches up in silence.

As the clients started coming in, they all looked at Peaches like she was a circus freak. Although they didn't say two words to her, fear of making her feel uncomfortable, they all knew something really terrible had happened and when she was ready to share her story, it would come flowing out... someday. Well, today was the day because as soon as Mrs. Howard, the woman who can't keep anything in her mouth but spit and food, came in the silence was over.

Mrs. Howard was known for gossiping and saying whatever popped into her head anytime she felt like it.

She had no filter. Mrs. Howard strolled in, took one look at Peaches' face and gasped.

"Oh my God! Child, what woman tore into your ass for fucking with her man? Oh, don't act like you don't hear me with your nose turned up in the air. I know what I see and that looks like the ass whooping of a woman scorned or a man." Mrs. Howard snapped her fingers two times in a circle.

Dee shook her head at her longtime client. "Mrs. Howard, Peaches was mugged. Please hang your jacket in the closet and have a seat in my chair." Dee felt like she was chastising a kid.

Although she had hit the head on the nail, Mrs. Howard was suddenly embarrassed about her outburst. "I'm sorry, baby. Are you okay?"

Peaches didn't answer. She was still not ready to explain anything to anybody. She knew it was going to be hard to keep the lie going if she started giving details. She simply couldn't take the chance of fucking up somewhere and then having to tell the truth of what really happened to her.

How would I look telling everybody my husband kicked my ass because I cheated with a bitch, she thought. As she ran the sad truth through her head, she was brought back to reality when the salon door swung open. When she looked to see who it was, she turned her head as fast as she could.

"What's up, Peaches?" G-mama caught a quick glimpse her. Peaches tried to ignore her by zeroing in on her client's head. She waved her hand quickly and whispered, "Hey G," and focused on sewing her client's weave.

She didn't want G-mama to see her face, so she kept

her back to the shop and didn't turn around for shit.

After she finished her client, Peaches walked to the bathroom with her head down so she couldn't feel the stares of everyone in the shop and so G-mama couldn't see her face or her tears. However, that didn't work. When G saw her face see immediately looked at Dee nodded toward the bathroom and mouthed to G to go check on Peaches. When G got to the restroom she knocked on the door. There was no answer.

"Peaches, it's G. Are you okay? Peaches?"

G opened the door. Before Peaches could push it back closed, G was already in.

Seeing the bruises and busted lip up close sent G reeling. "What the fuck happened!" G screamed. "Who did this to you?"

"I was mugged," Peaches cried.

"Awwwww, don't cry." G-mama softened her tone the minute she saw the tears cascading down Peaches' face. "Are you okay?"

G-mama really wanted to put her arms around Peaches to comfort her, but she wasn't sure how she would react. Unable to fight the urge, G pulled Peaches into a warm, comforting embrace and to her surprise Peaches did not protest. She fell into G's arms and flooded her shirt with tears.

"You're okay, you're okay. Shhh. Calm down." G rubbed her back and cried with her.

Peaches knew she had to tell G-mama the truth because Rob would be looking to put his hands on G too. As G caressed Peaches and held her close, Peaches start telling her what really happened.

Meanwhile, Biggie was walking from the store when she saw someone busting out the windshield of Peaches' spray painted, keyed up truck. Biggie ran into the shop.

"Peaches! Where Peaches?" Biggie screamed, somewhat out of breath from running.

Dee jumped up in fear. "She's in the restroom. What's wrong?"

All the clients were in an uproar.

"What's going on?" Some of the clients asked each other looking from under dryers.

Biggie ran to the restroom just as Peaches finished telling G her story. As she opened the door slightly, not wanting to startle Peaches after what she already has been through, she peeked in and saw G-mama and Peaches kissing like long lost lovers. She took a deep breath to keep herself from screaming. Biggie couldn't believe her eyes. *What the fuck was really going on here?*

She stood there in shock for what seemed like forever. Then she slowly backed up from the door, closing it quietly behind her.

As she shook off her disgust, she thought to herself, *I knew it. These two always beefing and protecting each other, driving me and Dee crazy as hell every day with their nonsense.*

Now what else is Ms. Peaches hiding?

She didn't know, but she sure as hell was going to find out.

CHAPTER 7

"Objection!" Jeremiah threw his hands in the air to disagree with the cross examining of his client.

The judge denied it. "Overruled. On what grounds do you wish to disagree with D.A?"

"There's no evidence that places my client on the scene at that given moment. All the witness knows is that she saw the two of them arguing twelve hours before the victim was shot. There was no weapon found. District is badgering my client under false pretenses," Jeremiah defended.

The D.A took a deep breath and began again. "I'll reframe my question. Mr. Lewis, after fighting with the deceased, did you wait around until he wasn't expecting it? And that's when you took him out."

The witness cried. "No! He was my friend. We had a disagreement as most friends do, but he also had enemies. I would give anything to get that day back, anything."

"Can we take a break, Your Honor? I'm not feeling very well." Jeremiah pleaded with the judge.

"What? I'm cross examining the suspect, Your Honor." the D.A balled out.

Just then Jeremiah threw up all over the floor and his notes.

"We're going to take recess. It's lunch time, so let's take two hours. Mr. Willard, go get yourself together and we will resume at two o'clock."

Bang! The judge hit the gavel as hard as he could into the plate.

Jeremiah walked toward the restroom to rinse his mouth out. He didn't know what was wrong with him, but he had been feeling crazy for the last couple of days. He could not figure it out. Maybe he missed Dee more than he thought. No. That wasn't it. Maybe she gave him something.

Jeremiah spoke aloud. "No! What the fuck can it be?"

"Hey Willard, you look like shit, man. What? You just got paternity papers or something?" a partner from his office joked.

"What! Dean, what did you just say?" Jeremiah looked up in shock.

"It was a joke. Hey man, you look awful. Don't you have that big case today? Jay, do you hear me, man?"

Jeremiah stood still, in a daze, looking off into space. "She's pregnant!"

Dean's eyes bucked. "What! Dude, who are you talking about? Who's pregnant?"

"My soon-to-be wife." Jay jumped up from the seat.

He ran into the gift shop of the building, picked up anything in there that had to do with babies, jumped on the elevator and pressed p2. He hopped in his car and took off to the shop. In his mind he and Dee were a happy couple.

He arrived at Heavenly Hands in no time. "Dee, why didn't you call me? I can't believe I'm going to be a dad. Thank you, baby. Thank you so much." Jeremiah said as he approached Dee's station.

Dee stood there in disbelief. *How does he know and why am I in this damn shop by myself? Is he gon' kill me?* That was all she could think about in the two seconds he spoke. Jay dropped down on his knees and placed his ear to her stomach. "Hey, little baby. I'm going to be the best daddy. You're never gon' want for anything. I'm never leaving you."

He looked up at Dee smiled and asked her if she was happy. She was afraid to speak. She didn't want to upset him while she was by herself. *Where the hell is Peaches? She was supposed to be getting her windshield fixed and coming right back, damn!*

He stood up and put his hands on each side of her face. She jumped at the movement and he instantly felt bad.

"Dee, I didn't mean to hurt you, baby. I love you. I just didn't want you to leave me."

Dee still didn't say a word.

Jay caressed her face and ears. Though his touch was scary, it still felt so good to her and she wanted to be able to share the moment with him, but she was so afraid.

Jeremiah continued. "Dee, we should celebrate. Let me take you to dinner."

"Ah, um… no thank you." Dee said with fear in her voice. "I have company coming over to my house and she staying for a couple of days."

He stared into her eyes for about five seconds, but to Dee it seemed like a lifetime.

Then he said. "Okay, okay. You let me know when you're ready."

Jay then leaned in and kissed her as passionately as he could. Everything inside her exploded.

"I love you, baby," he said as he leaned and kissed her cheek.

He then started kissing down to her neck, which was her spot. Dee just threw her head back, forgetting the truth just for a moment because it felt so good to be in his arms again. He pushed her softly against the station, grabbed her ass firmly and picked her up as he devoured her mouth. Her pussy throbbed to the beat of his heartbeat and was getting moist by the minute. His dick was as hard as rock candy and pressing into the seam of her panties. Her dress was over her hips and she was ready to let him take her away. He moved her panties to the side and slowly pushed his finger inside her and let her juices flow down his hand. He then removed it and licked his finger clean, loving the taste of her. He bent down and put his mouth over her pussy and hummed softly. Dee filled her pink sheer panties with her own juices.

As it happened, he lightly licked with his thick, firm tongue, which sent her into an orgasm she couldn't control. This turned Jay on. He loved the noises Dee made when she had orgasms. He then slid her panties off, unzipped his pants and released his rock hard dick. Dee's dress was clenched between her teeth. Tears rolled down the side her cheek as she desperately wanted him to give it to her so good like she knew he remembered.

Jeremiah looked her dead in her eyes in said, "I love you, baby. Do you love me?"

Just as she was about to speak, he placed one finger over her mouth, kissed her on her forehead, and pushed his dick inside of her moist, accepting pussy.

"Ummm, yes, baby. You feel so good. Jay, oh baby. I love..."

As Dee was about to say it again, Peaches burst in the door.

"What the fuck is going on?"

Jeremiah jumped back. "This is none of your business. Get the fuck outta here!"

"I work here. Get the fuck off her." Peaches stormed in hard.

"What the fuck did you just say to me?" Jay walked toward Peaches with his dick swinging back and forth.

"Don't walk up on me, nigga! You don't want to find your ass in jail for real." Peaches posted up like she would beat a mofo down.

"Jay, stop! She's right. You should leave." Dee rushed back to her senses.

"But, baby we—" Jeremiah tried to be calm.

"No! This is not what we should be doing or the place to be doing it. Now please leave. I need to get my head together."

Jay thought about it, smiled, and got his self together. He remembered he was due back in court in less than an hour.

"I'm gon' win you back," he said as he ran out and jumped in his car headed back to the court house.

"Dee, what are you doing?" Peaches yelled. "That mofo is crazy. Do you really want that mofo back and around your baby?"

"No, I mean, I don't know. I love him and he is the baby's father. It's just... he touched me and I lost it for a minute, you know?"

"Look, girl, I know how it can be when you love a mofo and they hurt you. You sometimes can't focus straight, but that dude is crazy as hell. Girl, you don't deserve to be treated like that. There are some women out here that do deserve what they get, but you're not one of them," Peaches said, speaking of herself.

Dee felt embarrassed. "Peaches, I know that. I know that, really. But I'm all confused right now and I have a lot of thinking to do."

Jay ran to the court room to find it empty. He turned to walk to the judge's chambers and found an angry first time young black judge standing right behind him. Although he was the same age as Jeremiah he was still the youngest judge in Cleveland. He stood there with his arms folded, his chest sticking out and glasses sitting on the end of his nose like he was an elder, his neat low haircut waves danced under the bright lights in the courtroom. The judge cleared his throat. "So glad you decided to return to the scene of the crime, Mr. Willard. You know when I said get yourself together I didn't mean for you to take a vacation."

"Yes, I know. I had something important to take care of."

"More important than your client that's on trial for murder? Oh please enlighten me." The judge chuckled and leaned back in his comfortable leather desk chair.

Jeremiah adjusted his $300 designer tie. "Excuse me!"

The judge sat up straight and placed both hands on his desk. "What? You don't understand by enlighten me?" The judge cleared his throat sarcastically. "I repeat, what was more important than your client on trial for murder?"

"Well, um, well you see, umm. You know, sir, I was—"

"Are you some kind of idiot or something, Willard?" the judge yelled.

Jeremiah was aggravated and struggled to maintain his composure. "No! I'm not. And please watch how you speak to me, with all due respect, sir. I do have a legitimate reason for my tardiness. My fiancé' is pregnant and I just found out. I ran to her, not paying attention to the time. Now, I'll take whatever punishment is due to me, but I will not tolerate no one disrespecting me."

The judge lifted his right eyebrow. "Are you

threatening me, counselor?"

"No, I'm getting an understanding." Jeremiah raised his eyebrow right back.

"Is that so?" The judge smirked.

"Yes, sir, it is!" Jeremiah's face didn't change.

The judge sat back in his seat again. "I want you in my office first thing in the morning. Do we have an understanding on that?"

Jeremiah *stood up and buttoned his suit jacket.* "Yes sir." He thought to himself *"Back in the day you know I was the man, I would've beat your ass, you were my flunky when I ran the streets. followed me to collage and law school, just because it took me two tries to pass the bar and only took you one and now you're a judge, you think you're the man."*

The judge stood up. "Oh, and Willard you better watch your ass. Don't get too cocky or I'll nail your ass to the wall without any drawls on."

Jeremiah walked away and punched a hole in the door after the judge was gone. He hated it when people disrespected him.

"Man, this motherfucker don't realize he was about to get choked. He is so lucky he's a judge and, and...Oh my God, I'm about to be a father," he thought to himself. *"Shit, I have to get my head together. When Dee and I get married I'm going to need to control my temper for the baby. I'm a family man now. Yeah, a family man. I like how that sounds.*

"Yes, I'm going to be a dad. I need a ring!" Jeremiah spoke aloud to himself.

"Ok now, Peaches, I don't want this to be an ongoing conversation. You can put your things in the bedroom upstairs to your right. The bathroom's not finished yet. I've been redecorating it and haven't had a chance to work on it lately, but it's completely functional." Dee gave out directions to Peaches as if she was at a bed and breakfast.

Peaches looked around like she hadn't been to Dee's house before. "Okay. Oh, and thanks again, Dee."

"Don't mention it, girl!" Dee said playfully, lightening up the mood.

Dee sat down in her sitting room on her favorite chaise. She had one upstairs and downstairs. She began to think about the fact that Jeremiah knew she was pregnant. But how could he? Was he that connected to the pregnancy already? She began to envision raising the baby all by herself. Shit, she can't even keep plants alive longer than a week. How was she going to raise a baby? She's always been really strong, though.

"Can I really do this?" she spoke aloud.

Jay is so crazy. How would he discipline their child? She started to get freaked out all over again. How a guy so full of passion could be so dangerous blew her mind.

"I know what I have to do. I have to ask him to give up his rights so he'll never hurt me or my baby."

Just as those words ran across her lips, the doorbell rang.

She looked up as if the door was in front of her. "Who is it?"

CHAPTER 8

Biggie kept playing back that disgusting kiss in her head.
She couldn't eat after seeing them together like that. But
she knew it all along. It was just different seeing it first
hand, all in your face.

I know Peaches is hiding something about what really
happened to her. Why wouldn't she want to tell her
husband, or go to the hospital? Why didn't she call her
husband to tell him she was staying at Dee's house for a
while? Or why hadn't he called her? They usually talked
all day. And why didn't she say anything about her car
being vandalized? But, most of all, how is it that
someone vandalizes her car at the same time she got
mugged?

"Um hmm. Oh, she think she's nickel slick, but I have
her penny change. My mama didn't raise no fool. I ain't
gone let this shit go until I find out the real on what went
down." Biggie spoke out loud as if she was having a real
conversation with someone. "Then I can let Dee know
she being played by that skank ass bitch. I know just how
to do it, too. Why don't I pay a little visit to hubby and
see what really goes on?"

Biggie used the door knocker that hung right under
the peak hole on the big heavy oak door.
"Who the hell is it?" Rob's voice was loud and firm.
Biggie jumped out her skin. "Oh, it's Biggie."
"What the hell do you want?" Big Rob snarled.
"Um, is Peaches here? She hasn't been to the shop and
we were worried about her," she blurted out, using

something to get him to open the door.

But Rob didn't give a fuck. "Naw, that Bitch ain't here and you better get away from my door before you get it like that bitch did."

Biggie's eyes widened. "Excuse me. Look, we're just looking for Peaches and we need to know if she's okay. I guess I'll just notify the police to see what they come up with."

Rob jumped up, grabbed the door and swung it open with a thrust that almost pulled Biggie inside.

"Come in." He looked like a killer. He face was blank, eyes dead and it look like he hadn't shaved or bathed in weeks

"Um, no thank you! I'm not trying to come up stankin'." Biggie backed up so he wouldn't snatch her inside.

Rob bucked his chest in all challengers mode. "I thought gay hoes had heart."

"What! Naw, mofo, you got the wrong one. Ain't shit gay about me, so you can cool it with that, for real, for real. Where's Peaches? What did you do to her?"

Rob looked Biggie up and down. "She's not here. She's probably with one of the other gay bitches!" He shook his head in disgust.

Biggie took a deep breath, ready to up pipe on him. "Look, I told you once and I'm not gone say it again—"

"Yeah, whatever! Peaches ain't here. I kicked her ass the fuck out."

Biggie squinted her eyes as if she was confused. She knew exactly where Peaches was, but continued digging for information. "Really, well have you seen her or heard from her?"

"No! And I don't want to," he yelled.

"What the fuck happened, if you don't mind me asking?" Biggie got tired of pussy footing around.

Rob was suddenly crying. "She cheated on me!"

Biggie was stumped. Here was a giant man in tears. She didn't know what to do so she nervously patted his back. "Awwwww, don't cry."

Rob, completely disgusted by all of Peaches' friends, said, "Don't fuckin' touch me. I'm a man. I don't need your sympathy."

"It's okay to be a man, but nobody deserves to be cheated on. I know how it feels. You give a man your all and he comes home and turns his back on you. But this is not about me." Biggie sat on the couch next to him in the chair.

She loved to see a man have his own chair like the man-of-the-house chair that no one else can sit in. It reminded her of her grandpa. She was there to get the story on lil miss pussy bumper, but when she saw how down in the dumps Big Rob looked, she couldn't help but feel sorry for him. She touched his hand to let him know she wanted to comfort for him.

"I'm listening." Biggie sat back.

Rob started slowly. "I had a video camera put in the apartment I got for her. You know? The one up the way?"

"Yeah!" Biggie shook head.

"Well, I've been having this feeling that she was cheating on me, and all my homies been telling me shit, but I didn't want to believe it. Anyway, I did it and when I saw the tape I went crazy. I couldn't believe it. It was a woman making my wife scream and call her name and she was enjoying it. What was I supposed to do? All my homies laughing, talking about 'nigga, that's what's up.'

But I don't need all that shit. I love my girl just for who she is, not all that freaky shit. You know? Can you pass me that bottle of Patron?"

"Sure. You mind if I have a glass?"

"I don't think you want this, Biggie. Plus, Peaches told me you don't drink."

"Yes, I don't, but I just need a drink. We've had a busy week." Biggie sat back hard on the couch.

Rob smiled at Biggie's tough but sweet demeanor. "Wow! Was it bad as mine?"

Biggie chuckled. "I can honestly say, yes it was!"

Biggie knew she was crossing the line, but she didn't care. She was going to find out the truth one way or another. "Okay, so then, what? Seriously?" She asked as she grabbed a glass off the small cocktail table on the side of the couch and poured herself a drink.

"Well, when I got into the house I… I lost it and beat the fuck outta her ass. I had to. She crossed the line. You know what I'm sayin'?" Rob exhaled.

"Damn, do you regret it? Dee and I felt bad, how Peaches looked for a sec…" Biggie's voice trailed off as she looked into her glass.

"Yeah, I kind of do. She could have gone somewhere else and been with anybody else. Why did it have to be a bitch? Do you know how that makes a man feel? It's like he can't pleasure his own wife and she had to get a bitch to do it. A bitch! Man, that's just something I don't condone. She fucked up big time. I gave her the world because I thought she deserved it! But, you know what really pissed me off? She tried to lie about it like I was one of these ofay niggas or something."

"Yeah, it's always the people you love the most that hurt you the most. My granny, my mom's mother, used to always say 'what makes you laugh, will soon make you cry,'" Biggie said in a low voice as she looked down in her glass.

Rob bobbed his head up and down. "That shit makes a lot of sense. Your granny sounds like a really smart woman."

"I always thought so." Biggie smiled at the thought of her granny.

Rob jumped up. "You know what, Biggie? I kinda feel like dancing."

"What!" Biggie swallowed hard.

"My bad. Did I say something wrong? It's just usually when me and Peaches have an argument or if I'm having a bad day we put on some of our favorite songs and we'd dance until one of us can't take anymore or we end up making love, which always seemed to work. Sad to find out it was all a big lie." Rob staggered in a tipsy man's walk.

"Whoa, easy there. Um, I feel so bad for you. I came to get information from you and now to find out all this. I would love to dance. Do you have any jazz music?" Biggie wanted to make him feel better so she accepted his offer.

"But of course. What you know about jazz? They say jazz is the heartbreak music." Rob smiled.

He grabbed the remote, walked up to Biggie, put his hands softly around her waist and let the music lead them across the floor. Biggie couldn't believe it. The dancing really made her feel better, after all that she had been through with her ex over the last couple of years. She felt like she could forget all the fucked-up shit he put her through, all the school time she spent trying to get ahead in life, and all the pain she'd been through in her life, period.

Rob thought to himself how glad he was not to be alone to think about what he was going to do about the kids, or to cry over his pain, or what he did to his wife. He always promised himself that he would never put his hands on a woman. His stepfather used to beat the hell out of his mother and he vowed to never hurt a woman like that. After seeing his mom get her ass beat for years, he feared that it would rub off on him and it came true. And his mom didn't ever do anything close to what Peaches had done to him.

Rob shook his head hard. Right now he didn't want to think about that. This moment, with Biggie, felt so good. As they moved from side to side, their bodies seemed to become one as if it was what life should be. In the heat of the moment Rob leaned in and planted a kiss on Biggie that made her soul shake.

"What the fuck are you doing?" Biggie jumped back and rubbed her lips.

"Oh shit! I'm so sorry! Please forgive me. I honestly didn't mean to do that. I just got caught up in the moment. Are you okay?"

"Yeah, I need to go." She grabbed her purse and headed for the door.

"Please don't leave. The kids aren't here and I don't want to be alone. I mean, at first I thought I did, but since you're here now, I know I don't. Can you please stay? I promise to keep my hands to myself. Scout's honor!" He put up three fingers.

Biggie laughed uncomfortably. "I don't think that's a good idea, Rob. I can't cross this line. Do you understand? We've bonded in a way we shouldn't have, and it's only because you're hurting. Also, I wouldn't want to hurt another woman like that. I am no one's rebound chick either, okay?"

"Yeah, I gotcha." Rob chuckled

He scratched his head and continued. "You're right. I shouldn't have done that shit for real. It was a mistake. But I must admit, I've always found you kind of attractive!"

"Kinda?" Biggie smacked her lips and smiled.

"I mean; you have a drive for life that I admire. Really!" Rob folded his arms in a jail pose stand.

"Wait, why are you telling me this?"

Rob exhaled and started walking toward her. "Because you should know that you are worth any man wanting you and I don't think you know that."

"Can you please stop walking up on me?" Biggie looked around, making sure she did not fall over anything while backing up from Rob.

Rob smiled. "I wouldn't be walking up on you if you weren't backing up."

She laughed uncomfortably. "Umm, hmmm. I see what you're trying to do and I'm not for this, seriously."

"All right!" Rob smiled devilishly.

Just as she turned to walk out the door he grabbed her from behind and pushed his body as close as he could, pulling her really close into him.

Biggie screamed. "Please, Rob, stop!"

He whispered in her ear. "Do you really want me to stop?"

She spun around to face him head on. "Do you really want me or is this your way of getting Peaches back. You know, fuck one of her girls since she did?"

"Damn! You gonna come like that?" Rob was suddenly pissed.

Biggie squeezed the words through her teeth. "I wanna know."

He didn't know what to say, because honestly it was both. He did want to pay Peaches back because that ass beating wasn't enough. But he really wanted to taste Biggie's pussy. She smelled so good and her lips tasted like apples. Shit, he was horny as fuck. But instead of telling her all that, he stepped in and picked her up by her waist. She wrapped her legs around him, wanting to resist the feeling, but was not able to. He leaned her against the wall and took over her mouth with his tongue. Both were moaning and groaning, panting and scratching each other. It was what they both wanted at that moment, but Biggie couldn't help but to think she was going below her standards. This wasn't her at all.

"Rob, stop. Rob, please stop!" she begged.

But he wanted her and he knew she wanted him just as much. He went down on his knees and pulled her down to the floor pulling at her bootleg slacks and kissing her stomach. She squirmed and pushed to try to get him off of her.

"Rob, stop!" she screamed, thinking she set herself up to get raped.

Her face was red and full of anger, not pleasure… anymore.

But Rob wouldn't stop. He wanted her to enjoy the moment just as much as he knew he was going to. But just as Biggie was starting to feel like she was going to have to bust a cap in his ass, he stopped.

"I'm sorry. Damn, I'm so sorry. I thought you were playing hard to get until I looked into your face. Look, you should go. I done fucked up the mood and I should not be doing this shit anyway. You're right. It's mostly for all the wrong reasons."

Biggie got up off the floor, gathered her things and left.

Rob flipped out and turned the house upside down. He wanted Biggie at that moment.

"I wouldn't be feeling like this if my scandalous ass wife wasn't gay as fuck." He said out of breath.

Biggie jumped in her car, wondering what the fuck just went down. She was enjoying herself until he became all rapist like. At least she found out the truth and now it was time to confront her bi-sexually challenged co-worker. Let's see what lies she comes up with now, she thought.

CHAPTER 9

Dee yelled out, "I said who is it?"

"It's me, baby," Jeremiah said through the door. "Can you open the door? I have something very important I need to say to you."

"Jay, what are you doing here? I told you I was having company." Dee yelled through the door.

"I know, baby, but this couldn't wait. Please open the door."

"Um okay, but no funny stuff. I'm not in the mood." She opened the door not knowing what to expect. To her surprise, there was Jeremiah, standing there with all the teddy bears, and baby items he had bought from the gift shop earlier.

Jeremiah smiled, carrying in all the gifts. "I got these things earlier. I meant to give them to you, but I had to find out if it was true. I was so excited I couldn't wait to get to you. Is there somewhere I can put all this?"

Dee's eyes widened. "Yes, you can put it on the table in the living room."

"Okay, okay. Look, baby, I know we've been through a lot and you were probably ready to write me off, but you know you can't now. We're having a baby, right? Well, I've been doing a lot of thinking since you've been gone and really since I found out about the baby and well..." Jay got down in front of Dee on one knee and grabbed her left hand.

"Jay, nooooo. Don't do this. You're not thinking clearly. We're not in a place where you should even think I would say yes to marrying you." Dee snatched her hand away from him.

Jeremiah was still on one knee. "Dee, I love you and I

want to be there for you and our baby. Please do me the pleasure of being my wife?"

Dee was stunned in disbelief at his actions, especially after all he had done. "Are you listening to me? I'm Can't marry you."

"Yes, you will. You're just scared now. You think I'm gonna hurt you again, but you don't have to worry about that. I'm gonna get some help with my anger." Jeremiah looked pitiful like a sad puppy.

"You are trippin'. Look, I must admit, I still have very deep feelings for you and now that we're having a baby, I mean, *I'm* having a baby..." Dee corrected herself, purposely to let him know she could do this on her own.

"What? What do you mean *you're* having a baby?" Jeremiah's voice was laced with anger.

Dee stepped back, rubbed her belly and said, "I just think we need to go our separate ways."

"What! You want me to just walk off from my responsibility?"

Dee stayed silent. She didn't want to get him all crazy, especially with only Peaches as her back up.

"Okay, okay. You're right. It's been crazy and I know I fucked up a lot, but please don't take my baby from me. I'll give you all the time you need. Just wear the ring for me and when you're ready to give me your answer, I'll be waiting, willing, and able to be the best husband and father that ever existed."

Dee had to admit that the ring was bling blinging. It was gold with a pearl setting in the middle and diamonds all around the pearl. It was a three-part ring set with band included. She was so impressed by it. They saw this same ring at an antique store in Aspen when they stayed at a cute little bed and breakfast for an entire weekend. She remembered loving it so much, but she wasn't thinking of getting married at the time. She just expressed her love for the ring and now as she stared at the brilliant diamonds twinkling, she knew that was it.

Dee couldn't believe he remembered and that he went back to Aspen to get it. She accepted the ring and decided to think about it. Although she already knew her answer, she didn't want the drama, so she promised she'd think about.

"Yes, yes you're going to think about." Jeremiah picked her up and kissed her repeatedly.

Dee pulled away and made it clear. "Yes, just think about it. But you know this means I need my space. You can't be pushing up on me because you feel like you want an answer when you want it, okay?"

"Gotcha!" Jeremiah said with a huge smile on his face.

He left Dee to her thoughts and smiled all the way to his car.

Dee watched as he left out the driveway. The minute he was out of sight she yelled out for Peaches.

Peaches came rushing down the stairs. "Yes, what is it? Are you okay? Did he hurt you? What? What's going on?"

Dee held her hand up. "No, better than that. He proposed!"

Peaches watched Dee's eyes gleam at the ring with pure glee. "What! I know you told him to stick his proposal where the sun don't shine, and kept the ring as you kicked him out!"

"Umm, no, not exactly." Dee squished her face like a child.

"Dee!" Peaches frowned.

"I know, I know. I just couldn't do it. For one, I didn't

want any drama. I still love him and he seemed so happy. I couldn't break him down. Not yet, but I will. I'm going to let him down, but easy." Dee held her hand up to the light. "Isn't it the most beautiful ring ever?"

"Yeah, it is fly." Peaches agreed hesitantly.

Dee detected the doubt in her friend's voice. "Peaches, I'm not tripping."

"Okay, okay." Peaches walked around the coffee table and plopped down on the couch. It hit her that she had her own problems to deal with, namely getting thrown out of her own home and being forced to live with her friend.

Dee watched her out the corner of her eye. "Now, are you ready to tell me the truth?"

Peaches took a deep breath, looked up with tears in her eyes, knowing she wasn't fooling anyone.

"Dee, G-mama and I have been messing around for months now. I don't know how it happened, but she makes me feel so sexy and beautiful. The more I try to resist her, the more she drives me crazy." Peaches began.

Dee's mouth dropped. "For real!"

"Yes. Well, she's been coming up to the apartment Rob got for me and I didn't know he had cameras up there and he saw us." Peaches broke down in a full blown cry for sympathy. But Dee was too shocked to give it at the time.

"You and G?" she said still in shock.

"Yes!" Peaches cried out in embarrassment.

"You and G, really?"

"Yes, yes, yes! Damn it, what do you want me to say, Dee? I'm gay? Well, I'm not. I just was trying something, but I didn't know how far it was going to go. I love my husband. He's a great man, husband, and he's the father of my kids. I love my children!"

Peaches looked into Dee's eyes to see if she was judging her or really trying to understand.

Dee was still in shock. "You and G? G as in G-mama?" Dee questioned once more.

Peaches was just about to answer when a loud knock at the door scared the pants off of both of them.

"Dee, it's me, Biggie. Open the door. I got something to tell you, girl!"

Biggie continued to bang on the door.

Dee ran to open it. Her heart was beating fast as she thought someone might be trying to hurt Biggie or something.

"Biggie, girl, what is it? Are you okay?" Dee rubbed her belly in fear.

"Yes. No. I don't know." Biggie was throwing her hands and arms all around. "Where is she? Where is that nasty bitch?" Biggie yelled, walking through the house trying to find Peaches.

"Biggie, calm down. She's in the sitting room." Dee followed Biggie through her house.

Biggie stormed that way, but Peaches was already meeting her at the door.

"Tell Dee what really happened between you and your husband. Tell her, you nasty bitch." Biggie accused as she pointed her finger at Peaches.

"BIGGIE!" Dee screamed from behind.

"No, Dee, you need to hear this shit." Biggie was sweating like an athlete.

"She already knows," Peaches said with gulp in her throat.

Biggie turned to Dee.

Dee nodded. "Yes, I know. What you are doing here?"

"Letting you know what the fuck kind of person she really is. She sits around dogging G-mama all day, belittling her and making her seem like this big ass freak when she's having an affair with her. On top of all that, you're letting her stay with you? When you were getting your ass beat the fuck down, she acted as if you were a strange bitch on the street."

"Biggie, I know you're upset."

"No, fuck that! I'm mad as hell, Dee. And you should be too."

"Well, I'm not, Biggie! I have to be here for her. *We* have to."

Biggie snatched her head back and forth. "Fuck that. I don't have to be shit, Dee. And neither do you."

"Biggie!" Peaches tried to reach for her.

Biggie moved away. "Don't touch me. I don't like you or trust your ass."

"Look, I know I've been a bitch, but I never meant for any of this to happen." Peaches started to cry again.

"But shit did. Fuck you and you too Dee. You condone this shit? Really? I'm outta here!" Biggie walked off.

"Biggie, wait." Peaches said as she fell to the floor in tears. "She's right. I'm a horrible person, friend, and wife. Rob could be out there right now looking for G-mama. What's wrong with me?" She sobbed uncontrollably.

Dee stood in the foyer with her hand on her forehead looking back from Peaches to the door, wondering what to do next.

CHAPTER 10

Jeremiah knew he had to make some moves and fast. He knew Dee would not really be willing to marry him, especially not with her girls at hand. He needed to get close enough to one of them to get into the mind of his beloved, but which one? Biggie was out of the question. That little firecracker almost had him 6feet under when he followed her and Dee to her house the other last week. Although he owed her an ass kicking big time, he knew speaking with her was not an option. Now Peaches seemed to be the one, but that bitch seemed cut-throat and he couldn't trust that she would give a fuck. This had to be put off on the weakest link.

Jeremiah smiled to himself. *The dyke. That homeless ass bitch was always looking for her next meal ticket.* "Hell yeah. That's it." He smiled and chuckled to himself as he looked for the business card with all the girls' numbers on it.

I'll just give this little dyke bitch a call to get in her head, he thought to himself. *And if she refuses, I'll dead the bitch.* I'll take all those hoes out of her life if I have to. Dee will be my wife.

G-mama was down in the dumps. She missed Peaches and needed to hear from her.

"Damn, I've left too many messages on Peaches phone. Why isn't she answering? I keep getting her voicemail. I hope she's okay. I can't believe that motherfucker did that shit. Damn, it's been a week now. Somebody got to know something." G-mama spoke aloud to herself.

Her phone began to ring. She quickly checked the caller ID but it was an unfamiliar number. She answered it. Peaches, is that you?"

"No, this is Jeremiah."

"What, what the fuck you want, dude?" G pulled the phone back from her ear in disbelief.

Jeremiah rolled his eyes in his head, wanting to check this dyke bitch, but he maintained his temper enough to get his words out. "I want to meet with you. I need to speak with you face to face about Dee."

G sat up in her seat. "What? Have you hurt her again? I swear motherfucker I'll find you and cut yo' balls off."

"Calm down, please. And watch your mouth. I can meet you." Jeremiah kept his composure.

G smacked her lips. "Hell nawl, fool! So you can try and kill me or something? I'm never that stupid."

"No, really, we can meet anywhere you want. I really want to talk to you about something important. I know you're Dee's favorite and I know she would listen to you. I'll make it worth your while."

G thought about it. She was broke and she could use a drink, so she agreed.

"Yeah, okay. Meet me down on 23rd and Rockwell at the Shake 'em up."

"What! That's a gay bar!" Jeremiah protested.

"Well, that's where I'll be, so if you wanna meet, you'll be there in a half an hour." G forced her hand.

This little dyke ass bitch has more guts than I thought, Jay thought as he hung up the phone.

As Jeremiah drove downtown to the club he got a sick feeling in his stomach. *Not only is it gon' be dyke bitches down here. It's going to be faggot ass dudes down here too.*

"All I know is if any motherfucka say shit to me out the way, it's going down." Jeremiah said out loud.

He pulled up in the parking lot, where a parking attendant was in the booth. He is wearing a pink curly wig, glittered bra top and matching skirt, with some white thigh boots.

"It's five dollars, boo," he said to Jeremiah as he popped his lips.

"Don't call me boo." Jay tossed him a $5 bill and then sped away with to find a parking spot. He parked as close to the door as he could, walked through the crowd of gays and into the bar.

"This dyke ass bitch better get here fast, because I don't know how much of this I can take," he said and rolled his eyes at the flaming gays who were staring at him.

He sat down at the bar, turned around, and G-mama was sitting right beside him.

"What!" she said as soon as they caught eyes.

Jeremiah jumped because it seemed like she came out of nowhere.

"Damn, where the fuck you come from?"

"I saw you come in." G smiled, knowing she shook his ass.

"Look, I just need to talk to you real quick…"

"Damn, a sister can't get a drink first?"

"What? Oh yeah, whatever." Jeremiah signaled for the bartender.

Down walks a six foot two, light skinned, teal eyed, skinny, but curvy dude. He was wearing a navy blue striped half shirt, a white layered tutu skirt, and some striped boots, with a hooker ponytail hanging down his back.

Jay was disgusted.

"Yes, sexy, what can I get for you?" the barmaid

chewed his/her gum seductively.

Jay rolled his eyes, looked at G and said, "What you want?"

G ordered her usual. "A Corona with a side of Grey Goose, the get loose juice, and ginger ale."

Jay held out a twenty. The barmaid grabbed his hand with the money and said, "And you, sexy?"

Jeremiah almost lost his shit. "Look, faggot ass moth..."

G-mama stopped him. "Hey, hey, hey. Look, you can't do this shit here. Look over there. You see that motherfucker with that gat in his hip? And up there, that motherfucker with his hand behind his back? You will get loaded with pure steel up in here. Shariff, get the drinks and stop playing." Then she turned back to Jeremiah. "Now, what you want to talk about?"

Jeremiah didn't really give a fuck, but he was there on a mission and decided to stay focused. He didn't want shit to go down in there and then he'd be on the news at a gay bar.

"Look, I asked Dee to marry me, and I need you and y'all other bitches to get on board. I know Dee not gon' do shit without y'alls approval."

G gave him straight attitude. "First of all, you have a lot of nerve coming in here asking me anything after the shit you pulled with Dee at our shop. And who the fuck you calling bitches? You know what? You high class mofos kill me thinking you should have everything you want 'cause you want it. Fuck that! I will never help my girl get killed by the hands of you." G-mama pointed her fingers as she was speaking, not afraid to let him know how she felt. Then she turned to walk away.

Jay grabbed her by the arm. The gunman in the corner

took two steps up. Jay quickly released his grip when they both caught eye to eye.

"Please, listen G-mama. I love Dee. She's carrying my baby and I know I need some help. I never want to hurt her again and I definitely would never hurt my baby. I'll do anything. I'm begging you for your help, please." Jeremiah took a wad of money out, grabbed G-mama's hand lightly and slid the cash into her hand.

"Think about it. Then give me a call. You have two day or I'm coming back for my money, or I'll be coming back for you." Jeremiah got up from the barstool and walked out the door.

Shariff watched him as he walked out. He licked his lips seductively as he strolled up to G. "Um, Ms. Thang, who is tall, dark and handsome? And why you letting him walk out our life?"

"It's not what you think, mama, not even a little bit." G turned around to the dance floor, thinking about what is being asked of her.

She loved Dee too much to ever mislead her to do anything that would put her in harm's way. *This motherfucker just laid two G's on me,* just as she was deep in thought, she noticed this chick on the dance floor whining her body to the view of where she was sitting. Although her mind was focused on so many things, Peaches being one of them, this bitch was sexy as fuck. The chick was touching herself and smiling at G.

G-mama turned around to see if she was aiming at her. Just as she turned to look back Shariff said, "Yes, it's toward you, honey, because fish is not nowhere in my appetite." She/He let out this loud howl. "I like it long, hard, and thick!" She smacked her ass then walked away.

G shook her head. That girl is crazy. She turned her

focus back to lil' Ms. Sexy, but she was gone. When G looked up again there she was right between her legs.

"I know you're not gon' let me dance out here by myself."

Ms. Sexy said to G.

"You're not by yourself. It's almost a hundred mofos out there with you." G shot right back.

"Yes, but none of them dance like you." G has been known to win competitions for dancing.

"Well, that's true, but I'm just enjoying the view right now."

The chick pulled G up from the bar stool. "One dance then." Ms. Sexy said. "You can enjoy anything you want."

G liked when chicks wanted her, but she liked the chase, not the pull. Shorty was hot, so she gave in. When they reached the dance floor sexy mama couldn't keep up with G's dance grind. G moved her all over the floor.

Ms. Sexy turned to her and said. "Damn, baby, you got me out here sweating, I know some other things we can do that keep the sweat up."

She took G-mama's hand and placed it between her thighs, rubbing her hand on the thickness of her warm pussy.

G was turned on, although she would rather have Peaches.

Shit, can't fuck the one you want; fake it with the one you're with, G thought. She turned Ms. Sexy around, pushed her over and made her dance the dog with her. The girl loved every minute of it. She rolled her body really close to G. "Don't you want to know my name?"

G replied, "No!"

"Why? I know your name."

G turned her around. "How?"

"I been watching you for a minute. I like you. I know you don't have a girl because I always see you by yourself, and I asked around."

G didn't say a word.

Ms. Sexy continued. "My apartment is close to here. You want to stay over?"

G grabbed her hand, never saying a word.

The girl took it as a yes and they both left the club.

CHAPTER 11

Biggie was pissed!

"Oh my God! How could Dee be listening to that lying, back stabbing bitch, letting her lay up on her like that? I can't believe this. Fuck this! I'm not gon' let her ass use my girl. Damn, this has been a hell of a day. I need a shower to wash off the hell of this day."

Biggie stormed into her huge, luxurious bathroom. She turned the water to run her a bubble bath, stood in front of her ceiling to floor mirror and undressed. As she took off her clothes, she thought of Big Rob's hands all over her. It lit her fire. Her nipples started to get hard and she felt her clit stiffen to the thought. She bit her bottom lip, shook off the thought and jumped in the shower. While the water cascaded over her body she couldn't resist the urge to touch herself.

"Stop it!" Biggie yelled. "I can't do this!"

But she couldn't stop thinking of him. Although she wanted it to stop, it couldn't. Her hands had a mind of their own as she rubbed soap over her breasts and down her six-pack stomach, then back up to her supple breasts. She moaned in pleasure. Biggie then rubbed her thighs together, trying to resist touching herself. But she needed to feel it. Her hands traveled down below and she rubbed and rubbed until she reached the pubic of her pussy under her bubbly water.

"Ahhh, damn. This shit is crazy. I can't touch myself. I feel so guilty, like I'm doing something wrong. This man has something over me. Here I am acting like some club ho, ready to pounce on another woman's husband," she said aloud to herself thinking it would stop her urge.

But her hands didn't stop trying. With bubbles

covering her legs, she opened her thighs just a smidge, then one of her fingers pierced the opening of her deepness. She couldn't stop what her body needed. She took one finger and played with her clit while inserting her middle finger deep into herself. Faster and faster she massaged herself, breathing fast and hard. It felt so good to her tears run down the left side of her eyes to her cheek. She then put one leg up on the side of the tub, took another finger in. Now with two fingers thrusting in and out of her wetness, she grabbed her right breast and rapidly pumped her fingers in and out of herself until she screamed in pleasure.

"Aaahh ahhhh ahhhhhh. Uummmm!" Biggie hollered as she came.

"Damn, let me wash my ass and get the fuck outta here. This shit is sick. I can't keep this up. He belongs to that bitch, but I want him so bad. How could I let that shit happen?" she asked herself, while feeling guilt and pleasure at the same time

Once she got out the tub, Biggie slipped her nightie on. She walked into her room, wrapped her towel over her head and sat on the side of her huge bed, with white linen covering it from top to bottom. She looked over at her phone, thinking about calling Rob. She shook her head, knowing it was a bad idea. Instead of grabbing the phone, she pulled the covers back, jumped in the bed and tried to get some sleep.

Two hours later, Biggie realized she was still awake and the throbbing sensation was still roaring between her thighs. She was still thinking of Rob. She wished it would be different and she could just call him. Just as she had the thought, her phone began to ring. She jumped.

"Ooww, shit. That scared the fuck outta me."

"Hello!" Biggie snapped to let whoever it was know she didn't appreciate them calling so late.

"Um, hey. Yeah I know it's late, but I just couldn't go to bed thinking you thought of me as a rapist."

"Rob, what? I mean, wow. It's crazy. I was just thinking um… well, it doesn't really matter. It's really late." Biggie couldn't get her words together.

Rob said with a sigh. "I know. I really wanted to apologize. I hate that I made you feel attacked."

Biggie felt so much softness in her heart for this man. "It's cool. You've been through a lot and if I felt like you really meant me harm, it would've went a whole different way."

He laughed. "Oh really?"

"Yes, really!" Biggie said with a little cuteness in her voice, mildly flirting.

"So are you in the bed?" Rob asked as he slid back in the chair.

Biggie reposition herself under her covers. "No not really just relaxing."

Although she knew that was a lie, she didn't want him to think he was interrupting her.

"Oh really. So what does that consist of?" Rob asked.

"What?"

"You relaxing?"

Biggie gave a cute girly laugh. "Oh, well I take a warm shower, put on my nightie, and then I lay across the bed with the TV turned to *Law & Order*."

"Wow, I guess you really know how to have a good time." Rob chuckled.

"Ha-ha, oh you have jokes, huh?"

Rob and Biggie laughed and talked through the rest of the morning. Before they both knew it, the sun was coming up and it was time to get their day started.

Biggie's alarm sounded off. "Oh my goodness it's seven already? Wow, it doesn't seem like we've been on the phone this long."

"Right. Honestly I can't remember the last time I actually stayed on the phone with anyone this long," Rob said with a stretch.

Biggie had to come back to reality. "Rob, you know this is not good, right?"

"Well, that's your second time saying it, so I'm sure I got it."

"I'm sorry. I just don't do stuff like this. Even though Peaches and I don't get along, I still believe in being a stand up ass chick."

"Look, baby, I understand, but I can't help being attracted to you. And it's not a rebound. I really think you're a sexy, smart, beautiful stand up chick. And honestly, we're not doing anything wrong, only talking."

"Yes, but—"

"Look!" Rob interrupted her. "Let's go have some breakfast. I mean, we're friends too, right?"

Biggie knew the answer to that but chose to stay quiet. Then she came up with an even worst idea. "How about you come over here for breakfast?" Just as the words left her mouth, she knew it was all bad from there, but finished her question anyway.

Rob smiled at the thought. "What's your address?"

"321 Neff Avenue." She couldn't believe she gave her address so easily.

"Oh yeah, I know where that's at. I'm gon' get myself together and I'll be right over. I should tell you, I don't eat pork."

"Biggie smiled. "Good, neither do I. Actually I don't

eat meat at all."

"Wow, that's different." Rob said, surprised at knowing someone who doesn't eat meat. "Well, I'm definitely looking forward to this breakfast. See you in a min, boo."

"Ok!"

As soon as Biggie hung up the phone she jumped out the bed and raced into the restroom to get freshened up. She tossed her nightie over into the hamper, washed and brushed, and oiled down her body. She then ransacked her closet, looking for something informal to wear, so it didn't look like she was trying too hard. She looked into the mirror, loving what her hair was doing.

She ran down to the kitchen to get her breakfast started. She took out some homemade croissants she'd made earlier in the week and froze just to have them prepared for bake and go. She took out her organic eggs, put on a pot of water for grits and grabbed a pan for some home-style potatoes.

Biggie grabbed the potatoes out the potato can to cut some up with onions, garlic and fresh parsley from her garden. She also cut some fresh fruit and squeezed some fresh orange juice. She took out her nice flower table cloth, put some flowers in a vase, and placed her plate mats on the table. She completed the table setting with crystal stemmed glasses for the orange juice, plates from her china cabinet and nice sterling silverware from her grandmother's collection. Her grandmother had been a maid to some old, rich white family and gave the silverware to her on the dying bed of their mother.

She looked over the table and smiled at how loving it looked. She loved to decorate and design so it always made her feel proud when she impressed someone.

She could smell the onions and garlic melt into the butter. The aroma flowed through the room. She placed the cut up potatoes into the sauté pan with the onions and garlic and placed the cover over it. She then turned to stir milk into her grits.

Just as she was taking the croissants out the oven, the heavy knock at her door sent quivers through her uterus.

"Who is it?" She yelled fast before the knock ended.

"It's me, Rob."

Biggie walked to the door, giving herself a onceover. She took a deep breath while opening the door with a big smile on her face.

"Hello!" Biggie smiled.

Rob was standing there looking kind of nervous. He was wearing a white tee that curved his big masculine muscular chest and arms, a pair of light gray jogging pants and some timberline boots. "Hey, what's up, ma?"

Biggie hated it when guys called her ma, but she let it pass because she already liked him.

She waved him in. "Please come in."

"Wow, this is nice," he said as he glanced around the room. "You decorated it yourself?"

"Yes, how did you know?"

"You said it when we were talking." Rob eyed her up and down.

Biggie smiled at the fact he listened to her and remember what she had to say.

"Impressive. You're a listener."

"Yes I am." Rob smiled, wanting to kiss Biggie on her lips.

For some reason, he was overly attracted to her, but he knew not to cross the line no more than he already had, so he just left it at that.

"So, what's for breakfast since we're not having meat?" Rob rolled his eyes in play.

"Well, I have some homemade croissants." She didn't bother to tell him she already had them frozen. "Some fresh fruit, home style potatoes and grits, scrambled cheese eggs, and freshly squeezed orange juice."

She led him into the kitchen as she described everything. "Well, you ready to eat?" Biggie asked.

He watched her walk around the island and licked his lips. "Yes, I am!"

Biggie shot her eyes up at him, using them to tell him to stop it without using words.

He smiled, and then walked behind her as she added fruit into a smaller bowl. She felt his body get closer to hers and it made the hairs stand up on the back of her neck. She had to tighten her thighs to hold in her juices.

"You can have a seat," Biggie squealed.

"No, I'll help you, if you don't mind." Rob's breath hit the back of her neck.

"Um I kind of do mind." She turned to look him in the face.

Wham! He placed a kiss on her straight on her lips.

She put her hands on his muscular chest, trying to stop him. Although she wanted it, she knew she had to stop herself. He wrapped his arms around her waist and lifted her up onto the island and it was on. They were like two animals, both tearing at each other's clothes. Bowls of fruit flew across the room. While it was on and popping, was she going to let this go on or was she going to stop it?

CHAPTER 12

Dee was too crazy in her mind, with all the bullshit that's been going on around her. She needed to get back into her shop tomorrow, plus its Monday and she has another Doctors appt. She also wanted to go talk with Biggie, she hated that her girls had beef, but more than that, her Biggie left her house mad at her, what was going on with this girl and she didn't know why.

Dee was going crazy. She wasn't sure if it was the hormones from the baby or the fact that there was unbelievable drama going down with the stylists of her beauty salon. It was bad enough her baby daddy was a nut case. One day he's an abuser and the next he's Prince Charming. One thing she knew for sure: her girls would not continue to have beef. The way Biggie left, pissed off and furious, was not like her. She had to figure out what was going on. Although she had a doctor's appointment, she needed to see Biggie first.

With her Michael Kors bags flung over her shoulder, she grabbed her keys and headed out the door. "Let me get over there, and once we talk and clear the air, then maybe I can get her to go to my appointment with me." Dee lifted one eyebrow.

Once Dee reached Biggie's driveway, she noticed an unfamiliar SUV

"Oh, Miss Thang has company. Well they need to get out because we need to talk."

Dee used the knocker to bang on the door.

It was too hot and heavy inside for anyone to hear anything. Rob had moved Biggie from the top of the island to the table. They were mid deep into grinding. They both fell from the table to the floor, which made a huge crashing sound. But they both didn't stop. With his finger inside her, Biggie was grinding her hips as he flexed his fingers in and out of her.

The loud noise scared Dee and she ran around the back. She moved slowly because she didn't know what was going on. But she knew she had to find out what that noise was. Her friend could be in trouble. She touched the door knob to see if the lock was off. As she turned it, she heard Biggie scream. Her heart stopped. She just knew her friend was hurt. But was the killer still here?

"Okay, Dee, get your game face on," Dee whispered to herself. "Where my knife at?" She quickly dug in her purse and retrieved her blade. "If he is still here I'm 'bout to cut him for asshole to appetite."

Ready to rumble, Dee snatched the door knob, rushed in and screamed out, "Get yo' hands off her, motherfucka!"

Rob jumped up. Biggie jumped up. And Dee was stunned. "What the fuck? Rob? Biggie, what are you guys doing?"

Biggie called her name out of breath. "Dee! It's not what you think."

Dee grabbed her belly in shock.

"You and him? No, no, no, no." Dee ran out into the backyard throwing up in Biggie's vegetable garden.

Biggie struggled to put her clothes on and ran after her.

Dee looked up at her with tears in her eyes. "How could you?"

"Dee it's not like we planned this. It just happened."

"No, this shit doesn't just happen. You're wrong." Dee ran to her truck. She had to get away from there. She didn't want to know this. She wished she hadn't seen it.

Dee started her truck.

Overcome with embarrassment and shame, Biggie walked back into the house, sat on the floor, put her head in her hands and cried.

Rob sat in the kitchen chair, feeling like it was mostly his fault. Biggie couldn't even look up at him.

Rob jumped up. "Hold up. Fuck that. I'm not sorry and you shouldn't be either. After everything that ho did to me." He got down on his knees in front of Biggie. She was still crying and sniffling. "Biggie, look at me."

"No, no I can't." She cried deeper into her knees.

"Biggie, baby, look at me. You don't have to feel bad about shit. I want you and I needed this and so did you. Come here." He pulled her into his arms and started kissing all over her face and her hands.

She wanted to resist, but she wanted him more now. The emotions wouldn't let her stop and the tears kept pouring. Rob grabbed her up from the floor, wrapped her legs around him and carried her out of the kitchen.

"Where's your bedroom?"

Biggie pointed in the direction of her room and it was on. Rob laid her upon the bed filled with white linen, pulled off all the clothes she had left, and pulled his white-T over his head, and his jeans down to his ankles. Biggie looked at his muscular form and gulped a big swallow. She looked at his down below and almost fainted.

"Wow!" She patted her chest.

Rob smiled at her amazement. He climbed onto the bed, kissing her from her feet all the way up to her knees, then up to her thighs.

Biggie couldn't think, see, or hear anything, as he moved closer to her deep sensation. She pulled all the breath into her lungs, scared as hell. She stilled herself. Then, there it was. He opened his mouth wide. She could feel his warm breath and then he placed his whole entire mouth over her deep moist sensation.

"Oooohhh, myyyyy, Gooooddd! Please..."

Rob kissed, tugged, licked, and sucked so softly on her throbbing fullness. Every move was gentle as he was careful not to be too aggressive to make her fear him in anyway.

Biggie trembled. She couldn't produce words with her mouth, a lot of noise was coming out, none of it made any sense.

"Yes, baby, what is it you want to tell me?" Rob says with a mere whisper.

He opened Biggie up and darted his tongue in and out, in and out, in and out of the moist juices between her thighs all the way up her ass and back up to her clitoris.

"Hhhaaa, hhhaa ooohhh, plea, umm, uummmm, ooohhh, sshh," were the only sounds she could muster up. She released all of herself into his mouth, and all over her sheets. Then in one flip he swooped her up and now she sat on his face. *Wtf*, Biggie thought to herself, trying to grab on to anything to maintain focus.

"Ride my face, baby. Damn, I want to taste you from this position," Rob whispered as he looked her directly in her eyes with pure lust and passion dancing behind them. "Damn, you're shaking. Are you nervous?" Rob asked.

"Yes, a little." Biggie smiled as if she was a teenage girl and this was her first time.

Rob pulled her face down to his, kissed her deep in her mouth and said, "You can do it." He pushed her up in the air and pulled her pussy toward his lips. "Now let me taste you."

Biggie got her grown man face on and rode that brother's face like she was in a rodeo. Rob sucked even harder on her clit than before, pushing his index finger into her ass and using his thumb from the front to play with her clit. She could feel her body trembling. She never came so hard in her life. She started bucking and jerking. It was so out of control. She thought she died for a mini second, because all the breath went out of her lungs and she couldn't hear, see, or think.

"Damn, baby. Oh shit, that was the best," Biggie said when all her senses returned. "How did you do that? I've never come so hard in my life. I've never had anyone make me come just from giving me head. You're a genius."

Rob smiled, but he wasn't finished. It was refreshing to have someone appreciate him like this, and he wanted more of it and more of her. So he flipped her over, dragged her down to the floor, pushed her legs over her head and pressed his dick deep inside of her pussy, grinding his hips deep into her, all with one thrash.

He sent Biggie's eyes to the back of her head with pleasure behind every stroke. With her mouth wide and pussy full, she was overwhelmed with the whole experience. She began to feel so much pleasure, then so much pain. A million thoughts ran through her mind. Who was she? Why was she enjoying having this beautiful moment with another women's husband? A woman whom she has broken bread with and baby sat her children? *Damn, this is the most amazing feeling*, Biggie thought to herself, *but also the most degrading.*

Was she who she couldn't stand? Rob noticed her moans faded away with worry and doubt crept upon her face. He wanted to stop, but he had already reached the point of no return. Tears began to stream down the side of Biggie's face.

"Aaahhhh, ahhhhhh damn, baby." Rob released himself deep inside her, fell over to her side, breathless. He reached over, lifted her head and gently wiped away her tears.

"Baby, what's wrong?" Rob asked Biggie with deep sympathy and concern.

"I see you like hoes..." Biggie balled, shedding tears in dismay.

CHAPTER 13

Once G- mama reached the well decorated apartment, she regretted ever agreeing to hook up with her. She only wanted Peaches, and now this bitch stood in front of her, looking at her with googley-eyed, like she was ready to fall in love and live happily ever after and shit.

"Stay right here. I'm gon' slip into something more comfortable. Would you like a drink?" Ms. Sexy offered.

Hell yeah, G thought to herself. But she just said, "Please," not wanting to hurt ole girl's feelings.

"The mini bar is around the corner, help yourself." Lil' Ms. Sexy smiled as she walked into what seemed to be her bedroom.

Moments later she came out wearing this one piece red teddy with the thigh highs to match and some red furry slippers.

"Missy!"

"What?" G-mama was unaware she came out the room.

"My name is Missy. You never asked my name and I'm telling you. Don't you want to know the name of your future?"

G-mama rolled her eyes in her head. "Look, baby, can we go out on the balcony? It's getting kind of warm in here, and I need some air."

Missy grabbed G's hand and led her out onto the balcony with the sexiest strut she could muster.

"This apartment is nice. So have you lived here long?" G asked as she took a sip out her glass filled with Grey Goose.

"Yes, well me and my ex lived here together, but she died, so now it's just me." Missy looked down to the ground.

"Dang, I'm sorry." G started to feel sorry for her. She immediately thought about how she would feel if that had happened to Peaches, who wasn't actually hers, but she loved her like she was.

Missy moved in closer, seeing G fading away into deep thought. She figured she was thinking of Peaches. Missy was determined to get that confused bitch out her mind. Yes, she knew all about G and Peaches. Missy had eyes for G-mama for a long time as she said. She would follow her around because she wanted to know everything she could about her. One time she followed G to Peaches' apartment and what did she find? Her soon to be boo slow grinding with Big Rob's wife. So she had a few of her boys who go to the same barbershop as Rob, plug him in on what was shaking, and poof, pow! Now her soon to be wife was standing out on her balcony.

Missy smiled, grabbed the glass out of G's hand, walked in front of her and kissed her lips— smooth and soft. G grabbed her in the back of head and pretended she was Peaches. She sucked her neck, down to her breasts. Although they were big and kind of hung low, she kissed and sucked on them anyway. Missy moaned because she believed all the passion G was giving was for her. G moved her thong to the side and played with her newly waxed pussy. Missy put one of her legs up on the balcony to force G to push her finger inside of her.

"Yes, baby, fuck me." Missy moaned.

G rolled her eyes. "This would be so much better if you didn't talk."

Missy started undressing G, kissing and sucking on her. G hated that, but she needed some pussy, so she let it go on. Before she knew it, she was naked as hell on ole girl's porch.

"Come on, baby girl, let's go inside," G said suddenly feeling uncomfortable that someone was watching them.

They walked inside, into Missy's bedroom and that's where the moans really ended. Missy had all kind of toys on the bed, straps, long dicks, short dicks, vibrators, butt plugs, nipple pinchers, handcuffs, and wipes. G hated using toys. More than that, she hated women who came on too strong.

This damn girl nasty ass fuck, G thought to herself. *She want me to use toys she used with someone else? Oh, hell naw. Where she think she putting this shit? She ain't planning on using this shit on me! I mean, I fuck niggas but that's real dick. I get it when I want it, not this shit.*

"I hope you don't mind. I brought out a few pleasures to add a little spice to this moment ." Missy smile and sucked on the small dildo.

G didn't want to put her mouth on this chick, let alone fuck her with already-been-used toys. *I'm here now, though, so I might as well get it over with.* She didn't even know what to use first. *This shit is crazy. Some bullshit ass toys.* She stared at the nipple pincher and laughed to herself.

G put her grown man on, slapped those nipple pinchers on Missy's hanging titties. Much to G's surprise the crazy girl loved it. She grabbed her, roughed her up, and flipped her over. She put the biggest dildo Missy had inside her wet, throbbing, nasty ass pussy and fucked her as hard as she could, pounding it to the bottom of her. Missy threw her ass right back into it, grinding her hips, and getting more and more wet. G couldn't believe it.

"Fuck me harder, baby. Umm yes! You're so good, daddy." Missy screamed out at G.

G, in shock, did as she was asked. She pushed hard, so hard her hand started to get tired. While she did that, she took a butt plug and shoved it into Missy's ass, thinking that might slow the nasty bitch down. But Missy moaned in pleasure and grinded her hips even harder.

"Umm, yes, baby. I knew sex with you was gon' be great. Please don't stop. Fuck me just like that," Missy said as she squeezed the nipple pincher tight.

G just kept it going, hoping Missy would get tired, but she didn't. It went on for about forty-five minutes. Then she came real hard, screaming and yelling as if someone was killing her. G was glad, but it wasn't over. Missy grabbed G threw her down on the bed, and start eating her pussy like a caged animal. She reached for a dildo to put inside G.

"Hey, hey, hey! What the fuck you doing? You're not putting that shit in me. You must be crazy."

Missy was bewildered. "Why, what's wrong?"

"Look, I don't play that shit!" G said with a stern voice.

"Oooh, I got you, daddy. You're all man right now. I'm sorry, baby. I will never disrespect you again." Missy smiled. She loved that G was taking a stud role. "Okay, well, take over, daddy. Fuck your pussy. I love the way you fuck this pussy."

"Shut the fuck up!" G pushed Missy back, actually tired of hearing her talk stupid.

G-mama gang fucked Missy with every toy she had out there, until Missy fell into a coma-like sleep. When G realized she was out for the count, she got up, put on her clothes, and ran up out of Missy's apartment, promising never to return again.

The next morning when Missy awoke to find no G-mama she was furious.

"Oh, so you think you're going play me like a jump-off, then run back to your little hair dresser? That bitch will never want you like I do. I'm Missy and Missy always gets what she wants. I ain't nobody's jump-off. You're going to be mine. And if I can't have you, no one will," Missy said as she stared into space and declared her love.

CHAPTER 14

Dee made it to her appointment a little early. She sat in the car to get her head together. She was in extreme shock. *What the hell had just happened?* She kept wishing it was a bad dream, because shit was getting crazier with every waking moment. Was she being punished for some reason? Maybe she was cursed. Whatever it was, only prayer could help at this point.

She closed her eyes and bowed her head in prayer. Suddenly she heard a tap on her window. She gasped. It nearly made her shit her pants.

She rolled down her window. "Jeremiah, what are you doing here?"

"It's your first appointment. I wasn't going to miss hearing my baby's heartbeat for the first time. Baby, what's wrong? Are you okay?" Jeremiah smiled like he was invited.

Dee needed someone to vent to and she couldn't believe he was here, let alone able to tell something was wrong with her just by looking at her.

"So much is going on, Jay. The girls are into it, the shop is in a uproar because of it, Peaches is staying with me because we don't know if her husband is gonna kill her, everybody's sleeping with everybody." Dee broke out in tears.

Jeremiah chuckled. "Damn baby, calm down. We don't want to upset my baby. Come on, let's go inside, get signed in, and you can tell me all about it. Did you eat breakfast?

"No, I was going to…"

"Hold up. You walking around here worried about some grown folks, and you're not feeding our child who is unable to feed himself?" Jeremiah stopped. He saw himself freaking Dee out. "Baby, I'm sorry. Don't make that face at me. I just worry about you and our baby, that's all. Come here. Are you okay?" He took Dee into his arms, held her close, and kissed her forehead.

Dee shook her head yes. She knew he was worried and she needed him right then, more than ever. With her friends all over the place, he was the only one she could depend on at the moment.

They walked in, and who did they walk into but Mrs. Hathaway with a basket of goodies.

"Oh my goodness. Look at you, you made the right choice and this must be that beautiful baby's handsome father." Mrs. Hathaway greeted them filled with country morning love.

Jeremiah and Dee looked around wondering what baby she was speaking of.

"Excuse me?" Dee asked, confused.

"Oh you know I know y'all baby gon' be a beauty because you're so pretty and he looks like he just stepped out of GQ magazine. I'm pretty good at this kinda thang."

"Well, if that is so, then yes I am the father. I'm Jeremiah." He extended his hand to the goodie lady.

She laid her hand in his and Jeremiah kissed it ever so softly.

"Well, my, my, he is a charmer." Mrs. Hathaway smiled at Dee, giving her a onceover, as if to say you're lucky.

Dee gave her a fake smile, thinking to herself *if you only knew lady. Now give me one of those cookies.* But she decided to wait till Mrs. Hathaway offered.

"Well, I'm sure you're hungry. God knows I'm always

putting something in my mouth." Dee and Jeremiah looked at each other and chuckled.

Dee said, "Not enough. This is her ninth baby."

Jeremiah said, "Oh yeah, she should've swallowed this one."

Mrs. Hathaway realized she was going on. "Oh, would y'all like some cookies or muffins?"

Dee reached up and took them both. "Thank you!"

"It's nothing. There's plenty more. How about you, kind sir?"

Jeremiah turned up his nose. "No thank you."

Dee was looking at him, as if to say *you don't know what you're missing*. She licked crumbs from the corner of her mouth and continued to stuff her face.

Jeremiah loved that he could be here for this moment, seeing Dee feed his baby made a warm smile appear on his face that he didn't even recognize.

The nurse called for Dee to come to the back. They both jumped up, but the nurse asked Jeremiah to stay out in the waiting room. "Excuse me, sir, you have to stay out here." The nurse held her hand up with an apologetic smile.

Jeremiah lost it. "What? I'm her fiancé and this is my baby. What the fuck you mean I have to wait out here? I want to hear my baby's heartbeat."

Dee's eyes widened. The nurse and the whole waiting room was silent. The nurse quickly pushed the button for security, but Jeremiah was already too upset to hear the nurse.

"Sir, sir, sir you have to wait out here until we get her prepped, and then someone will come and get you." Another nurse stopped the alarm and calmed the situation

Dee was embarrassed with tears pooling in her eyes.

Mrs. Hathaway left her goodies in the waiting room, grabbed Dee and walked her to the back.

"Aw, it's okay, sweetness. My husband was the same way— overly excited and not aware of the circumstances.

Dee didn't even look back at Jeremiah. And he knew why, even if no one else didn't.

Jeremiah put both hands to his forehead. "Please excuse me, everyone. This is my first child, and she's stressed out, and I don't know the rules, and I never been here before…"

Before he could finish, two huge security guards were coming out the elevator. "Sir, please step back."

The nurse put her hand up to stop them. Feeling sorry for Jeremiah, she told them it was a false alarm. She got Jeremiah some water and told him to take a deep breath.

Meanwhile in the back that nurse wasn't fooled. She knew something wasn't right so she took all the extra precautions. "I have a few questions for you," the nurse said as calmly as possible, as not to offend to Dee. "Number one, how do you feel about this pregnancy? Number two, do you feel safe at home? And finally, are you sure this is what you want or are you being forced into it?

Dee almost fell out her seat in shock. *This bitch is for real.*

Dee took a deep breath. "I mean, I know this situation that just happened was a lot, but are you for real?"

"Ma'am, we have to ask these questions, just to be sure you and your baby are safe." The nurse darted her eyes directly into Dees direction, to see if she could see fear in her eyes.

"I'm happy to be pregnant. I wasn't sure when I first

found out, but I love my baby and I wouldn't change this for the world. Yes, I feel safe at home. I live alone. My fiancé sometimes gets over active (she found herself defending Jay), but he loves me and our baby. No, I'm not being forced into anything by anyone." Dee rolled her eyes, but understood about the nurse was simply doing her job.

The nurse finished up, put Dee in a room and sent for Jeremiah.

When the doctor came in the room he said, "I hear we had a situation, dad." He smiled at Jeremiah as if he understood. "It's fine. It happens all the time in here. We've actually had worst."

The doctor came around in front of Dee with her legs in the stirrups and sat between them. This made Jeremiah uneasy, but he held his composure, well until, the doctor pulled out this long ass, dick-looking object. Then it was over.

"What the hell is that and where are you putting it?" Jeremiah eyes bucked.

"This is so we can see the baby and hear the baby's heartbeat, sir," the doctor explained.

"Calm down, baby." Dee rubbed Jeremiahs' hand to reassure him. And it worked. He calmed down instantly.

Watching the doctor the whole time, Jeremiah was almost disgusted at the thought of him putting that shit up in Dee, but as soon as he heard the baby's heartbeat, all of that was gone. Light bumps echoed in his ears.

"Oh my God." Jeremiah smiled. "That's my baby, my baby's heartbeat. Tears ran down the side of his face. "Can we see him… or her? I'm cool with that too."

The doctor pointed to a circle on the screen. "This is your baby."

Jeremiah was so excited he kissed Dee over and over. "I love you. Thank you. Thank you so much. I promise I'm going be the best father and husband."

At that moment, Dee believed it was true. "I know, baby."

Jeremiah looked up at her. "So... that's a yes?"

Dee smiled, crying and caught up in the moment. "Yes, it's a yes."

The doctor cleaned Dee up and stepped out the room, while the happy couple shared their joy. Dee dressed and cleared her mind. *What have I just done?* Am I really about to marry this man? I need my girls right now, but they were all over the place. *God, if this wasn't it, give me a sign.* Nothing happened.

"What are you thinking about, baby?" Jeremiah was beaming with happiness.

Dee responded, "My next move..."

CHAPTER 15

The next morning, after Dee spent the whole day and night at Jeremiah's, she went to open up her shop. It was like she had missed a month in there. She opened up the blinds and checked the voicemails. There were calls from everyone. Clients were wondering what was going on. "What happened up there?" "Did someone die?" "I need my hair done. Are y'all still opened?"

Dee rolled her eyes in her head, are we still open? "Hell yea. Wow people were really scared that we were gone shut down, this shit is crazy, a lot has happen." Dee talked to herself some more. "But it's nothing I can't fix. I have to get my girls back, right? But how? If I knew how I wouldn't be talking to myself."

A voice from behind her said, "And why are you talking to yourself?"

"G-mama," Dee said excitedly, "I didn't hear you come in."

"Apparently," G said while stepping into Dee's wide open arms for a hug. "Umm, Dee I have something to tell you, but before I do I want to make sure ..."

Just as G was going into her story, in walks Biggie. She had her head hanging low. Dee hadn't seen or heard a word from her since the day she walked in on her and Big Rob rolling all over each other.

"Hey, y'all," Biggie managed to say in a low voice. She was still embarrassed and avoided looking directly at Dee or G-mama.

Dee's eyes followed Biggie to her station then stopped as she settled into her chair.

G, not aware of the situation with Biggie and Rob, sensed something was up. She mouthed to Dee, "What happened?"

Dee rolled her eyes and shook her head, not wanting to ever speak on it. She walked to her station and awaited her clients.

G-mama shrugged her shoulders.

As the clock rolled around to 9 a.m. the door swung open and Paula, one of the craziest clients to ever come through the shop, strolled in.

"Wwwhhhaaaasss up? Damn, y'all alive? What? Y'all had a shop vacation and forgot to tell everybody? What happened? What it is, what it look like, what it do?" Paula laughed and through up the peace sign on both hands.

"Now Paula how you gon' come in here with your head looking like you just got outta two dog fights, asking us questions?" Dee replied.

"Oh, yes. I know, right? Well you know my boo thang spent the week wit me and we christened the house, the restaurant, my car, his car, the park, and three of my neighbors' back porches. I mean, killing it." Paula whined her hips in a circular motion. Then with one leg hiked up to the side, she stuck out her tongue.

"Aaaahhhh. Girl, you too crazy." G killed herself laughing. "Now please tell me how the hell you fuck on three neighbors' back porches."

"Shit, he asked for it. I thought it was a little rude myself, but girl, he holding so serious. He could've told me to fuck in the neighbor's bed and I probably would have." Paula hit G-mama with a high five.

"Is it he holding or your ass is that freaky?" Dee asked with a smirk of real talk in her voice.

Paula grinned with an innocent look and said, "Yeeess!" in her baby voice. "You know how I do?" she continued in her ghetto voice. Then she slapped G a high-five again and laughed.

"Y'all two are definitely two of a kind," Dee laughed.

"Right. But my homey G-mama is hitting off the mofos and the bitches." Paula said, slapping G another high-five.

Just then G-mama's phone rang and the caller ID showed restricted. "Damn, here we go again." G exclaimed in frustration.

"What?" Dee peered.

"Someone has been calling my phone all night and morning hanging up."

Dee said concerned, "And you have no idea who it is?

"No, Dee, I don't. It's been restricted every time."

"Oh shit! Yo, yo, yo... I'm telling you, you might have a fatal attraction," Paula said with the most serious face the shop has ever seen her with.

"What? No." G brushed it off. "It could be some kids playing on my phone. I have been doing a lot of advertising lately. They probably found my card and just being kids with nothing else better to do. I'm not too much worried about it, just tired of it is all."

Dee cleared her throat. "G-mama, it could be Rob." She hated to say it, but it had to be said.

Biggie shuddered at the sound of Dee even saying his name, as if everyone knew her dirty little secret.

"Dee, don't say that." G felt a sinking feeling in the pit of her stomach.

"Why not, G?" Dee went in. "He fucked Peaches up already. He said he was gon' get you too. He could be looking for you."

Paula looked from one mouth to another. "Wha? What happened? What? What he do to Peaches? What? What y'all do? Aw damn, y'all. You think he coming right now? Hey, that door locked? Man, I'm too young to die." Paula went crazy really quickly.

"Dee, look, I don't think that's it. As a matter a fact, don't even say that." G said, although she knew what Dee was saying could be true. Rob could be thinking about coming after her. He was crazy, flat out, but he was not the type of mofo to play on a phone.

Just as G went into deep thought, the door swung open again. This time it was another mofo on G's bad side. Her eyes widened and she then remembered what it was she needed to talk to Dee about.

Biggie couldn't believe it. *What the fuck was he doing here and with flowers and shit like shit sweet?* She thought.

Jeremiah walked into the shop with arrogance in his swag, purposely to let the girls see him stake his claim. He was moving his way back into Dee's life.

Biggie jumped up from her station. "Dee, I know you're trippin', right? You can't possibly have forgiven this mutha—"

Dee stopped her in mid-sentence. "Umm, you need to worry about your own affairs, Ms. Thang, before you check me on mine."

"Whaat!" Biggie snapped her neck in anger. "Girl, you know this muthafucka is crazy as hell and you're about to sit here and act as if he just didn't beat your ass weeks ago. Dee, what are you thinking? Come on."

"Biggie, this is none of your business." Dee held her hand up to stop her girl for caring about her well-being. "Now, please stop it." Dee felt sad about checking her friend, but she needed to let her know her decision was just that, her own decision.

G-mama was so angry, but too stunned to get into what Biggie and Dee were talking about. G stared at Jeremiah with pure anger in her eyes. He stared back as if to say "you better not say shit about the money I gave you, and bitch you better have my money."

Just as Dee turned her attention back to Jeremiah, Biggie grabbed her bag and walked into the back to clear her head of all the foolishness.

The door to the salon swung open and in walked a young city worker who had been working outside on the sidewalks.

"Damn!" Paula shouted out at the sight of a 6"2, white boy with a tan and a bright smile, his flexed muscle peered through his work vest and dirty work jeans, "Who that be?"

"Hello, ladies. My name is Trouble. I work for the city and we've been working down the street for the last couple of weeks and now I'm down here near your shop, so I wanted to let you know we're pulling up the ground right here and around the corner."

"So you're gon' block our shop with that big ass machine?" Dee was not happy.

"Well, not right at this moment, but yes, soon enough." Trouble said, trying to ease the tension.

"Wait, y'all tearing up our sidewalk? How are our clients supposed to walk in?" Dee walked to the door speaking loudly but not being ghetto.

"Just let us know how many clients you have today and if it will pose a problem. I'll make sure we wait it out till tomorrow." He came back with a solution.

Trouble smiled. He was feeling the way Dee showed her frustration with class, but also he always had a thing for black women, and Dee had a glow that just did something extra to his manhood.

"I'm sorry, ma'am," he said. "But if you let me know how long your day will be today and tomorrow I'll try to work with you. I will start around the corner first, then work my way back around, but it has to be done this week."

"Whatever." Dee walked away.

Jeremiah stepped up. "Hey, just do what you need to do, but you can do it without the smile on your face. What the fuck you smiling at anyway?"

"Nothing, sir, just a man of joyful days. I love to share my happiness," Trouble said and turned around and walked out the door.

"Girl, that mofo was fine. Did he say he gon' be here all week?" Paula licked her lips. "G, come on and get my hair done. I think I got jungle fever. I know he does." Paula said while looking at Dee.

G-mama was listening, but she wasn't at the same time. She knew she needed to do something and fast.

Jeremiah turned his attention around to his new fiancé, rubbing her stomach. "Baby, are you okay? Is my baby hungry?"

Dee smiled. "No, we're fine."

"You sure baby? Don't be upsetting my baby now." Jeremiah pushed.

"We're fine, baby, really."

Jeremiah continued. "I love you, Dee. You know this, right? If these motherfuckers fuck with you guys too bad, let me know. I can make a few phone calls and get it together for you."

G-mama was losing her mind. She panicked just as Dee was about to open her mouth to say the words back to him. "I lov…"

G interrupted. "Look, here's the money you gave me the other night, Jeremiah, I can't do this."

Jeremiah could've shit on himself. He couldn't the bitch was playing him right now.

Dee's eyes bucked. "WHAT! What is it you can't do?"

Dee's eyes shot back and forth back from G-mama to Jeremiah. Her mind stormed with thoughts of only the foulest images she could think of. Tears welled up in her eyes and she was ready to go crazy. She grabbed the money out of Jeremiah's hand. "This is almost two thousand dollars! You paying for pussy? Paying for pussy from my home girl? What the fuck?"

"Dee," G pleaded. "What? You have it..."

"Shut up! You dyke-ass bitch. This is how you play me, G- mama? I have always been there for you, had your back and this is how you gon' do me? Get the fuck out my shop."

Paula was amazed. She couldn't believe what was happening right before her eyes.

"Dee!" Paula interrupted.

"Shut up." Dee checked her quick.

"Dee, stop. I would never play you like that. I'm doing this for you," G-mama tried to explain.

Dee slapped her with so much might, it knocked G to the floor.

"Daaammmmnnnnnn!" Paula shouted out in shock.

"GET OUT!" Dee screamed, as tears rolled down her face.

G-mama rubbed her cheek, which still stung. She got up off the floor with the help of her client, Paula. She shook her head sadly, knowing in her heart she would never hurt Dee. Rather than make the situation worst, she grabbed her backpack and her hat and walked to the door.

"Come on, Paula. I'll do your hair at your crib."

She turned and looked at Dee with disdain. "Dee, I hope you know what you're doing and when you find out the truth, you know my number."

She walked out the door in tears and didn't look back.

Dee fell to her knees. She loved G-mama like a sister and to find out she would play her like that destroyed her from the inside out.

Jeremiah dropped to his knees with Dee. "Baby, what are you thinking? Do you honestly think I want that chick?"

"Get your hands the fuck off me and get as far away from me."

Jeremiah tried to explain. "Baby, Dee, please don't do this. Let me explain."

"Get outta here!"

"Dee, I called G …"

Just then Biggie walked out from the back, saw Dee on the floor and lost her mind.

"What the fuck! Dee, you okay? Get your hands off her."

Dee jumped up and ran in the back in tears.

Biggie pointed her finger in Jeremiah's face. "Look, the best thing for you is to get the fuck out of here or not only will you lose your life, I'll make sure you're never found again."

"Dee, Dee!" Jeremiah called out and tried to follow Dee to the back.

Biggie jumped in front of him, praying G- mama had her back. "I said leave."

Jeremiah knew fucking her up wouldn't be what was needed at this point. Plus, it would be horrible publicity for the firm, so he left.

Biggie looked around for G and Paula. She wanted to find out what happened, but, of course, they weren't there. Biggie threw her hands up, took a deep breath, and walked to the back to take care of her pregnant friend.

Biggie thought, *Damn! This has been a hell of a month. What next?*

CHAPTER 16

G-mama drove through the city, out the city and back in again. She was so upset, mad even.

"G, what the fuck just happened? How you gon' let Dee bitch slap you like that? What you do for that two piece, G?" Paula finally broke the silence in the car.

"Nothing, I didn't do anything, and I should've done something," G said in extreme tears.

"How the fuck Dee gon' play me like that? I would never do her dirty. Shit, only if I had told her sooner, before everybody came in the shop. That way when he walked his shaking ass in there, smiling like a Chester cheetah cat, it would have been his ass getting smacked to the floor instead of me." G rubbed her sore face. G-mama still was in full tears.

"Say what?" Paula asked.

G's phone rang. She glanced at it real quick and saw it was restricted again.

"Yo! Who the fuck is this!" G-mama spat, trying to shake whoever was shaking her.

A scary box voice said in evil tones, "Bitch, it's your worst night mare. You think you can play me like a sucka and get away wit it? You living yo' last days ho! I'm gon' get you one way or the other." The haunting laugh echoed in G's ears.

G looked at Paula. "You heard that?"

"Hell yeah!" Paula yelled in fear.

G was mortified. She wondered who was playing with her. Was this a joke? Was Big Rob really after her, or was it Jeremiah? She looked back and forth around in her rearview mirror.

HONK! A loud horn from the car behind her made her

jump and slam on the gas so hard she left tire streak lines in the street.

"Oh, shit. Damn, I thought they had me." G chuckled to herself. "Whoa. I'm tripping too hard, for real. Let me get myself together. I have no time to be tripping. I need to find out how to get Dee to listen to me and get her away from that psycho."

"Um, yeah. That's cool. You do that." Paula stared at G like she was from another planet. "You know what? You can let me out right here. I'll get wit you later about my hair, okay?" Paula jumped out the car and waved back to G. "See ya."

"Damn. See ya." G tooted the horn. She was a little surprised that her longtime client bailed on her.

"Peaches!" Biggie called out from the front door of Dee's house.

"Peaches, help."

Biggie walked Dee in through the foyer to the sitting room. Peaches came downstairs.

"What!" Peaches said with mad attitude, because it was Biggie calling her.

When Peaches got to the bottom of the stairs she saw Dee was in pieces with her mascara smeared all over her face from crying, she was weak and pale in the face. "What? What happened? Are you okay? Is the baby okay? What's wrong?"

"Peaches, stop screaming. She's fine. Something happened at the shop today with her, Jeremiah and G-mama." Biggie gave short details in-between breaths.

"G-mama?" Peaches instantly felt ashamed when she heard G-mama's name.

When Biggie saw the shame on Peaches' face, shame began to come over hers also. Although she couldn't stand Peaches, she had love for her. Thoughts of what she had done were all up in her stomach. Consumed with guilt, she could no longer look at Peaches.

"Dee, what happened?" Peaches bowed down in front of her.

Dee took a deep breath. With tears running down the side of her face she began to explain. "Jeremiah fucked G."

"What?" Peaches roared with laughter.

Biggie even chuckled a bit.

Peaches smiled. "Dee, are you crazy? No way did that happen. First of all, G is not even that type of chick who would do that to you or anyone."

Biggie instantly started to shrink, thinking *I'm wasn't either, but I did it with to you.*

Dee looked at Peaches. "She did it to Big Rob and you."

Peaches sat back on her feet and sighed. "Damn, Dee, that was different. I know G better than any of you might think, and I know she wouldn't do no shit like that. She loves you too much. Now tell me the story. Let me try to make sense of it all."

Biggie stayed quiet. As far as she was concerned there was no use in opening her mouth too much and letting any skeletons fall out.

Dee took a deep breath again and recounted what happened. "Well, we got to the shop. G came in behind me, then Biggie. After a client came in, then Jeremiah showed up. I saw in G and Biggie's faces they were upset, but I thought it was because of all that happened. Anyway, next thing you know, G comes handing Jay like two-thousand dollars. She said, 'here go yo' money back. I can't do it.'"

"So she said just that I can't do it?" Peaches asked with concern on her face.

"Yes!" Dee said with attitude.

Peaches put both hands up in surrender to calm Dee down. "Ok! I'm just trying to get to the bottom of this, because I don't think it's what you're thinking. Hmm, I can't do it."

"Shit it might be he wanted to have a threesome with her and some skank. I don't play that shit, so maybe he paid her to get that together for him, before we get married. Um hmm. Or, or maybe he paid her to tell me. Or maybe they had a threesome wit a man. He could be a down low brother," Dee said, jumping up off the couch

"Dee, stop it. You going crazy." Biggie shook Dee by her arms.

"Let's take a moment and think. This G-mama. She do her thing, but it's just that—her thang. She wouldn't want him or no one else in her business. Look how long they kept their secret," Biggie said pointing at Peaches. "No offense."

"None taken. It's true." Peaches got over the shame to help G's honor.

"Well, whatever the fuck it is, I know I'm done with both of them and that's that." Dee rubbed her belly, feeling sick to her stomach.

She stood up and headed upstairs to her room where she laid down across her bed and balled her eyes out until she fell asleep.

The girls let her be alone for the time being. Peaches immediately went into planning mode. "Look, you should go look for G. I'm gon' try to call her."

"What! Why I can't call her and you go look for her?" Biggie wasn't feeling Peaches giving her orders.

"Because I know she'll answer my calls and she would tell me exactly what happened. She's been calling me like crazy and I haven't answered her calls, trying to work through this shit. Look, I'm not trying to tell you what to do but I know her. If anything, she's back at the shop, probably picking up all her shit just so she don't have to tell Dee what the truth is. And knowing that motherfucker, he probably tried to use G-mama or manipulate her in some way. And we all know G would rather for the truth to come out on its own, than to be a snitch in any case." Peaches had her hand on her hip and phone in the other hand.

"Okay, you're right. I'm gon' go to the shop. You call her. Whoever come up on something first get proof, but make sure to keep in contact. Deal?" Biggie stuck her hand out to shake Peaches hand.

"Deal." Peaches returned the gesture.

CHAPTER 17

"Damn, I know those hoes in there making me look like a sucka to Dee," Jeremiah said as he sat outside her house.

Just as he started to flip in his mind Dee's front door opened, and out walked Biggie.

"Look at that bitch, probably going to get some shit, so she can come back and her and that other bitch Peaches can talk Dee into cutting me out her life." Jeremiah shook his head and started his ignition. "Let me get outta here before she sees me and tells Dee I'm stalking her."

He put the car in drive and drove away. As he drove through the city he thought to himself.

"Damn, I love Dee. What the hell is she thinking? Me and that dyke bitch fucking, really? I don't understand what would make her even think that stupid shit. Fuck! And that dyke bitch gone play me? Hold on. Wait a minute. Ha-ha, I can't believe it. There goes that bitch right there. I should kill that bitch."

Jeremiah pulled over as he saw G-mama come out the ma and pa store on Euclid Ave.

~~~~~~~~~~

As Biggie pulled up to the shop, she noticed a car sitting outside. She didn't know if it was G-mama or not because she rents different cars so much. She hadn't noticed what she was recently driving.

"Yes, she's in here." Biggie said with excitement in her voice.

She opened the shop doors and walked inside. "G! G-mama, are you in here? Damn, I guess not. I'll just sit and wait. She might roll around in a minute. Oh I left my book bag here, didn't I? Cool I'll just work on some homework and maybe wait to see if she rolls through."

"Um hmm, excuse me." A voice came from the front door.

"Whoa, shit!" Biggie jumped.

"Whoa, whoa. I didn't mean to scare you. Is G-mama here?" A very sexy, well-groomed young lady with an evil look in her eye asked. She was wearing a red lace long sleeve off the shoulders shirt, and a short black mini skirt, with cheap black sling back sandals. Some junk jewelry, and her hair was in a silk wrap.

"No she's not. Did you have an appointment with her?"

"Umm, something like that. Ooh, is this her station?" the sexy lady asked as she sat down without invite.

"Yes it is and since your hair looks all in place, I figure you're one of her groupies. Well she's not in and we're closed for the day. If you'd like to leave your name and your reason for coming, I'll tell her you stopped by." Biggie felt a way about this little skank.

The sexy young chick smacked her lips, got up with her mini skirt hiked up her behind. She seductively pulled it down and smiled. "No, no. I'll find her and give her what's coming her," she said as she walked out.

Biggie paid her comment no attention. She watched the young chick walk out the shop, hop into her car and pull off.

"G-mama has to find better taste in women. I hate to say it, but Peaches is the best chick she ever messed with. Umm hmm."

~~~~~~~~~~

While G took time to walk up Noble road thinking and looking in and out of the stores and salons, her phone rang again. "Oh boy, not again. I don't have time for this shit." She was getting sick of the childish phone games. As she contemplated turning it off completely, the phone continued to ring. She answered without even checking the caller ID. "Look, muthafucka! You want it? Come get it…"

A sweet, familiar voice stopped her. "Hello? Hello, G, are you okay?"

"Peaches? Damn, you called me back. What's up?" G was happy to hear her voice.

"What's up with me? What's up with you? What the hell happened between you and Dee and yuck, Jeremiah?" Peaches went in, not wasting any time.

G closed her eyes. "Maannn! Peaches, if I told you, you honestly wouldn't believe it."

Peaches smacked her lips. "Well, try me."

G cut her off. "Wait, where are you? Damn. Why are you just calling me now? Man, I miss the fuck outta you. How you just gon' cut me off like that and not let me know you're okay or nothing?"

Peaches took a deep breath. "G, you don't understand. A lot had happened and I lost everything… my husband, my house, and my kids. Shit, my dignity too."

G sighed. "Damn, you still could have said something. I love you, Peaches." She paused. "And we were friends before any of this shit went down. I'm sorry this happened, but a lot has happened with me too. Don't you care?"

Peaches felt G-mama's pain. "Yes, of course I care. It was just too much for me. Please try to understand. I'm calling now. We have to get to the bottom of this for you and Dee's sake. So tell what really happened, because I know you and I know you wouldn't play Dee like that."

"Well, it's like this." G began to explain how Jeremiah called her wanting to meet up. As G goes on and on, Peaches could not believe her ears. She always thought Jeremiah was too good to be true. He seemed sneaky and what G was saying confirmed it.

"…Then he pulled out his money, pushed it in my hand and walked out. You can call down to the club and asked Shariff. She was standing right there," G said.

Peaches chuckled. "First of all, Shariff is anything but a she, honey. And second, I don't have to ask anybody anything. I know you wouldn't lie to me."

G smiled. She was glad to hear someone was on her side. Just hearing Peaches' voice made her day one hundred percent better.

"Damn, this car is riding slow as fuck across the street. If I didn't know any better I would think it was following me." G was scared.

"What? G, what kind of car is it? What's going on with you G?" Peaches was worried.

"Man, I really don't know. I been getting these harassing ass phone calls and the shit got me shook for real, Peaches."

"Damn, who do you think it is?"

G shrugged her shoulders. "I don't know. Big Rob!"

"What? No way. He's not that type of man." Peaches exclaimed.

"No. Big Rob is coming out the barber shop. Oh shit, Peaches he spotted me." G almost shit her pants.

Peaches didn't know what to do. "Oh shit, run G."

G turned to run. "Oh no. The car is still right there."

Just then she noticed the window in the car was down and she was being followed by Jeremiah.

G was stuck. "Peaches, it's Jeremiah."

Peaches was so afraid for her friend and lover. "Damn, G, where you park at?"

G was out of breath. "Hold on, Peaches. I can't hear you. I'ma dip in this alley way."

"Now, what you say Peaches?" G asked out of breath. Peaches!" a voice came from behind G.

G-mama turned around slowly, blinked two times.

BOOM!

"Whew, G, what the fuck was that? G? Hello! G! G-Mama." Peaches began to scream out of her mind.

Then, in the background, she heard a dreaded voice disguised by a voice box. "Now, bitch, there won't be a next time for you to play nobody."

Someone fumbled with the phone. The voice said, "Is this Peaches?"

Shocked and completely terrified, Peaches dropped the phone instantly.

"OMG, Dee! Dee, you gotta wake up, baby." She shook Dee out of her sleep. "Something happened to G!"

Dee turned over with a groggy voice. "What? I know. I kicked her ass out my shop. Peaches, what's wrong wit you?"

Tears ran down Peaches' face. "Dee, I think someone just killed G. Get the fuck up. Now!"

Dee watched Peaches as panic set in. The hysteria in her actions shook down in Dee's soul. "What! Peaches, what you are saying to me?" Tears rolled out from her now awakened eyes. "No, no, no. Call her. Peaches, are you sure? What the fuck are you saying to me right now?"

"Dee!" Peaches grabbed her pregnant friend.

"Dee, please listen to me. I heard it all, okay? See look, we were on the phone and I was trying to find out what happened. She broke it all down to me and then she saw Big Rob."

"I knew it!" Dee cried out.

"A minute later she saw Jeremiah." Peaches shivered in her teary voice.

"Jeremiah? Oh no, Peaches," Dee whispered.

Peaches shook her head trying to get Dee to listen. "I heard a big boom and then this voice picked up the phone and they knew my name."

Dee was hysterical. "What? He knew it was you on the other end of the phone? OMG! Shit, you think he's coming for you? Jeremiah wants me to himself. He might just try to take all of y'all out to get to me. Peaches, I'm scared."

Peaches calmed down instantly. "Don't be scared, wait let me call Biggie."

"Peaches, hey you spoke to G?" Biggie answered her phone, relieved to see something might be in motion.

"Biggie!" Peaches cried.

"What? What's wrong?" Biggie was making her way out the shop to her car, thinking only the worst.

"I think G's dead." Peaches whispered through the tears.

"What, what the fuck you say, Peaches?" Biggie shook her head because she had to be hearing things.

"Well, I was on the phone with G, then she saw Rob, and Jeremiah was following her, then there was a voice and Biggie they knew my name. I think he's after us. Dee's scared and..." Peaches ran it all down in one breath.

"What? Who knew your name? Peaches, y'all calm down. I'm on my way. I can't understand what you're saying to me." Biggie hung up. She frantically locked up the shop, hopped in her car and took off full speed to get to Dee's house. As she flowed through the city she saw a lot of fire trucks, ambulances and cop cars heading up the way.

"What the fuck going on now? she wondered.

Before Biggie got to the house, Dee's phone began to ring Mary J.

Dee gasped.

"Dee, don't answer that phone," Peaches protested.

"But Peaches, he could be outside or have something to tell me. Shit Biggie's on her way here. What if he hurts her? At least maybe I can distract him. Maybe." Dee was all over the place.

"No. Fuck that. He can say some shit that might upset the baby. What if he says he gon' kill you or something? No, no, no." Peaches was wandering in circles.

"Peaches!" Dee shouted. "Let me handle this."

"Hello? Jeremiah, why are you calling me?" Dee said with fake confidence. She was scared, but she needed to feel him out.

"Baby, I know them hoes over there filling yo' head with all types of bullshit, but don't let them ruin what we're trying to build. Look, it's about us, our family and those hoes ain't a part of that. I'm a successful lawyer and you're a savvy business woman. We can make it together. Let me get rid of them hoes and show you that I can be the man you want me to be."

Peaches held her head close to Dee's head so she could hear what was being said on the other end of the phone.

When Jeremiah said that, she grabbed her mouth, crying. "OMG, OMG! He killed G-mama and now he coming for me and Biggie."

Dee hung up the phone because if he knew Peaches

was listening he might be on his way.

"Peaches, stop crying. Stop it. I need you right now. We need to find out where G mama was and see if she's actually okay. Then we need to find out our next move. I know you loved her and I know you're scared, but if we're going to get through this we have to do it together. Let's turn on the news. Maybe breaking news can tell us something." Dee was trying to be strong.

A knock at the door caused them both to scream. Then they heard Biggie's voice.

"What? Are y'all okay? Open the door. Someone in there?" Biggie started twisting the door knob in maniac mode.

Dee went to let her in. "Biggie, did you see or hear anything?"

"No." Biggie rushed in and locked the door behind her. "Now, what is really going on?"

Just then Mary J began to play on Dee's phone again. They all looked at the phone in silence.

"Dee, don't answer that phone," Biggie warned.

"Dee, answer that phone, if you don't want him coming after all of us," Peaches protested.

"Dee!" Biggie shook her head no.

"Dee!" Peaches' eyes grew in size three times.

The phone continued to sing.

Dee broke out in extreme tears. She couldn't hold back. So much was going on and she felt overwhelmed. "Stop it, stop, stop, stop! I can't do this. One of my best friends may possibly be dead, murdered by my child's father and fiancé. I may be having Satan's baby. He might be outside the house right now, ready to take y'all out one by one and me too if I don't side with him. And he might just get away with it, being the lawyer I know he is."

Just as she was about to finish, breaking news on the TV interrupted her. Still crying, panting, and sniffling, she sat on the cocktail table in front of her 55-inch television set.

"In Cleveland a young woman's body was found in a side alley way on Noble road early this evening…"

As soon as the reported stated the words, all the girls broke out in tears.

"The woman has not been identified, but nearby pedestrians state they heard a gunshot, then allegedly they saw a person walk not run out the alley way and down the street. They're not saying if the suspect was a female or male, but we'll have more when we come back."

Biggie jumped up, wiping her tears away. "Come on y'all. We have to get down there. We can't let her be blasted on TV with strangers."

Dee couldn't move. She sat there with tears rolling down her face. "The last thing I said to her was get the fuck out my shop."

"Dee, stop it." Biggie rubbed her shoulder.

"It's all my fault. I allowed her to go be murdered," Dee cried louder.

"No. Stop it. Stop it now. Look, shit might be crazy, but no one needs to be blaming themselves. This isn't about you and G or Jeremiah or whatever. Our family is laid out in some alley way while strangers all around her and no one knows her name or anything and we have to make sure the police know what happened to her. Now get up. You too, Peaches." Biggie shouted in anger to the situation.

Peaches sobbed with tears, she shook her head no. She

was overtaken with sadness. "No, Dee, it's not your fault. It's mine. Had I answered G's calls sooner she would have been here with us. Jeremiah or no one else would have been able to get to her."

"Stop it, damn it. Both of you get the fuck up and come on, now!" Biggie grabbed her keys and purse and stood at the door waiting.

CHAPTER 18

When the girls arrived at the scene police were everywhere. Yellow tape crossed the pathway and people were standing around looking and pointing.

Peaches' legs began to get weaker and weaker the closer they got to the alley.

"Excuse me, ladies, you can't be over here. This is a crime scene," the young officer warned.

"We're family. I mean, we think that's our family back there." Biggie could barely get her words out.

They all held each other's hands as they looked over the young officer's shoulder, trying to get a better view.

"Oh, well hold on. Let me get my sergeant." The young officer walked away.

He approached an older cop who had salt and pepper hair and wore pleated pants, a white pressed shirt and a jacket adorned with several medals. The young officer whispered in his ear and the sergeant turned around and shook his head in sympathy. Both men walked back over toward the girls.

"Ladies, I understand you think this may be a family member. What is it that makes you believe this to be true?" the sergeant questioned.

"Because Peaches was on the phone with her when she heard a gun fire and we haven't spoken to her since." Dee spoke up.

"You were on the phone with her? What is her name?" the sergeant asked with doubt.

"Savannah Georgia Howard." Peaches began to shake in panic as she recalled to the police sergeant exactly what happened.

He held up G's ID and stared at the girls. Before he

could say a word, Peaches hit the ground.

"Nnnnoooooo! Oh my God! No. No! OMG... OMG!" Peaches cried out in so much pain and agony.

Dee and Biggie consoled her, but their tears were heavy also.

The girls sobbed and yelled so much that the crowd began to cry. Although most of them didn't know G, just seeing a family in so much pain made it too sad for some of them. A woman murdered in broad daylight was too much for the community to bear. Some of the bystanders began to walk off in tears, women and men.

The coroner came over and cleared his throat before speaking. "Excuse me. We need you ladies to identify the body."

The crowd that was left became angry. "Don't make them look at that," one lady yelled.

"Y'all shouldn't do that here. Don't you see they're in enough pain?" a young man said from behind an older woman.

The girls seemed to be in a dream as they walked back into the alley. The crowd standing around was yelling, but the girls heard no words, no sounds. Although they were moving slowly, it seemed they were floating. The crowd was there but with no faces.

A woman yelled, "Be strong! God will punish whoever did this."

Peaches rubbed her eyes look into the crowd with a blank stare. Then she looked away and then back at the crowd again."Big Rob!" she whispered

What if Jeremiah didn't do it? Big Rob was pissed at G-mama too, and he's here. Before the gun shot she said he caught eyes with her. I can't think about this right now.

Damn, this is a moment I never thought I would be in, identifying a body. It's almost like waking to my own death. My stomach's shaking and my legs feel like rubber bands. I didn't know this many tears lived inside my eyes, Biggie thought to herself.

Dee began to pray in her mind. *"Father of God, please lead us through this alley with the strength and ability to view this body and not lose our minds. Father, I ask you to please take care of G because she is an angel. Father, please watch over my girls because I now know they're all I have. Father of God, please forgive me for what I did to G-mama and let her know I'm so, so sorry... in Jesus' name I pray. Amen."*

When the girls reached the body they were still holding hands and they gripped each other tighter.

The coroner pulled back the sheet and there laid G-mama with a gunshot to the head. Her eyes were still open and a look of fear and shock was displayed on her face.

"Why did this happen to her?" Peaches questioned. Tears rolled so fast down her cheeks she couldn't wipe them fast enough to stop.

A police detective stepped toward the girls cautiously with his notepad in hand. "Is this your family member, ladies? One Ms. Savannah Georgia Howard?"

"Yes, that's her." Biggie sighed.

Peaches fell beside G-mama's body. "G-mama, I'm so sorry. I wish it was me laying here. I just want you to know I love you, and I apologize for all the pain I caused you. And I, I... oooh God. Aaaahhhh, G, you were a good person. Wwwhyy they do this to you?" She turned to the detective. "Put her hat on, pleeeaaase. She like when her hat is on right."

Biggie and Dee grabbed Peaches by the arms. They dragged her away from G kicking and screaming. Their tears ran so heavy they couldn't see an officer coming to grab Peaches up off the ground and lead them to a patrol car.

"Ladies, we need to go to the station to answer some questions. Do you think you guys can do this?" the officer asked with sympathy in his voice.

The girls couldn't answer. They were pale and numb. Biggie opened the patrol car to help Peaches in who was still screaming in pain. Then she helped her pregnant friend, Dee in the car she was so limp she seemed bony and frail.

Once at the police station, the girls set cuddled up on each other waiting to be questioned. They barely said one word to anyone, not even each other.

"Would you ladies like some coffee or water?" A female officer, approached wearing glasses that sat at the end of her nose like Mrs. Claus.

"No coffee, but water for her. She's pregnant. "Biggie pointed at Dee.

"No, I don't want anything," Dee muttered.

"Dee, you need to eat something. You haven't eaten in hours and the baby needs something, even if you don't want it," Biggie fussed.

"This baby is part of a man who possibly killed G-mama. I don't want to feed it, carry it, think about it. I don't want this baby!" Dee cried.

"Dee, you can't mean that. Please calm down." Biggie comforted her.

"Peaches, drink something, please," Biggie begged.

But Peaches didn't answer. She stayed cuddled under Dee and looked far into whatever world she was in, wishing it was all just a dream. She desperately wished things were different.

"Ladies, please follow us to the conference room," An older father-looking investigative detective asked. Once seating uncomfortably in the conference room he said, "I'm so sorry for your loss and I know this is a difficult time, but if you know anything, or who may have done this, please let us know, so we can find the suspect." The detective looked at them all.

All the girls started talking at once, sounding like chickens.

"Whoa, whoa, whoa, one at a time. It seems you ladies have a lot of information. This is good. Any leads will help us apprehend the suspect and hopefully close the case much faster and much easier. How about this? We'll interview you all one at a time. That way we get everyone's story and then all together." He sat down and looked at them to see who wanted to go first.

"No, we don't want to be separated," Biggie spoke first.

"I understand, but if you all have something to say that could be used as evidence, this is how it has to go. We can't have all of you clouding each other statement. I promise I'll make it as quick as I possibly can so we can get you ladies home to start whatever preparation you need."

Dee said, "Oh shit we have to contact G's aunt and the rest of her family."

"Okay, you can do that while one of the other ladies goes first," the detective offered.

The girls looked at each other and hugged. Since Peaches had the most connection, she went first. The other ladies stepped out the room and started the family calling process.

Dee touched the screen of her phone and realized she had 25 missed calls all from Jeremiah.

"Look." She showed Biggie her phone.

Biggie was too much in her phone staring at all the calls she had from Big Rob.

"What? Oh shit. Dee, you have to get him down here, if you tell him where you are, you know he will come. Then the police can arrest him right where he stands. For real if they don't, I will kill him myself." Biggie started rocking back and forth.

Dee didn't know what to do. She loved Jeremiah, but hated him at the same time. As she dialed his number, all the anger inside turned into tears of mass destruction as soon as he answered the phone.

"How could you?" Dee blurted out.

"How could I what? Baby, where are you? I've been calling you all day. I just saw you on the news. What the fuck happened? Are you in trouble?"

Dee looked at Biggie to calm herself.

"No, I'm at the police station. I think I need a lawyer." Dee humbled her cry, mad as hell.

"I'm on my way, baby. Sit tight," Jeremiah said.

Dee hung up the phone.

"What? What he say?" Biggie questioned.

"I can't believe it. I see it on TV and movies all the time… people killing people and acting all normal. But to actually experience it in real life is crazy. This muthafucka acting like he don't know what's going on. This shit is crazy! I almost lost my mind, but since he wants to act I can too. I'm gon' make sure they throw the book at his ass too!" Dee cried out.

The detective was a 20-year vet who had seen and

heard just about everything, but when he questioned Peaches he received an earful and needed a coffee break, twice. He wasn't ready for the information he got…

Dee kept it strong when she called everyone. So many people were calling her after seeing it all on the news. After she called one person that person called someone else and then the next person would call her. By the time she thought she was finished explaining, people were popping up at the police station in tears and full blown cries. A lot of them were there for support.

The detective calls Biggie in, and then Dee. They each told their stories and had the detective's ears ringing. Although a lot of the information would be used as evidence, he knew when he played the tapes back for his team, they were gonna get a big kick out of some of the stories he heard tonight.

"Ladies, your story just might help a lot. Dee, make sure you let me know when your gentlemen friend arrives. Please let us handle it. You ladies need to go home share what you told me with each other and maybe you can bring it all together with things you couldn't remember. It bring up new evidence. If that does happen, give us a call a.s.a.p." The detective advised.

Just as the detective was letting the ladies out the conference room, Jeremiah walked in. "I'm looking for my fiancé."

Dee turned to the detective and said, "He's here."

"Excuse me, sir, what's your full name?"

The counter officer already informed if Jeremiah comes in he is to be arrested at once.

"What? I'm attorney Jeremiah Willard," Jay said, passing the officer his card.

"Sir, please place yours hands behind your back. You

are under arrest."

"What? Arrest me? You got me fucked up." Jeremiah struggled with the officer.

Three other officers came in to help.

"Get your muthafuckin' hands off me." Jeremiah was going off.

The officer began, "Sir, you have a right to…

"I am the law. I know my rights. What is this about? I'm here to pick up…" Jeremiah struggled.

"Sir, please stop resisting arrest." The officer was still trying to place handcuffs on Jeremiah.

"Wait a minute. This has to be a misunderstanding. I didn't do anything." Jeremiah continued to jerk his wrists away from the metal handcuffs.

Just as the cops finally got the handcuffs on Jeremiah, Dee walked up to him with tears in her eyes and anger in her heart.

SMACK! Dee slapped him! "How could you? How could you murder her?" Dee stared the accused in the eyes.

"Baby, what the fuck are you talking about? Murdered who?" Jeremiah seemed confused.

"Motherfucker, you know who." Biggie spat as she came out the room next.

"I didn't murder no motherfucking body! Hey, get off me! Dee, Dee, I didn't do this shit. Hold on. Hey, Dee! Dee, baby, you got to believe me."

The officers dragged him down the hall and into the investigation room. They threw him in the chair and shut the door behind them.

"Have a seat. You're going to be here for a while." The desk officer said while walking back down the hall.

The girls walked out with the police. They climbed

into the patrol car and the officer took them back to Biggie's car on Noble Road. Once Biggie was safely inside her car the officer pulled off and the ladies headed back to Dee's house to get started with the funeral arrangements.

CHAPTER 19

The girls reached Dee's home and they stayed up all night discussing what they all told the detective. Peaches was still crying her eyes out, but managed to tell Dee everything G told her about what went down with her and Jeremiah.

Dee couldn't believe her ears. "Why would he do that?"

Then Dee thought back to the day at the shop. She remembered G telling her she had something to tell her, but then people started coming in and that's when shit got crazy.

"Oh, shit! Paula. We need to call Paula. She left with G that day and she might know something." Dee started remembering shit just like the detective said.

"I don't have her number," Biggie cried.

Peaches was up on her feet, looking in her bag for her phone book. "I have it. I had to do her hair for G one time and I wrote her number in my book, because she always got the hook up on something. Hold on." She flipped through her book, "Oh here it is. 216-555-8817."

Dee grabbed the house phone and called Paula's number.

"Who dis?" Paula answered crazy as usual.

"This is Dee. Paula, are you busy? We need to talk."

"No, I'm not busy, just finished getting my hair done."

"By who!" Dee challenged.

"By this chick from the hood. She do hair out her kitchen. I know its ghetto, but hey, I had to shake G. She has some seriousness going on, you know?"

"What do you mean, Paula? Wait, you must not know." Dee took a step back.

"Know what?"

"About G-mama. She's… she's… been murdered." Dee broke into tears all over again like it was her first time hearing it.

"What? No, no. Please don't tell me that. Yo, for real, for real?" Paula's shocked voice hurt Dee's heart.

"Paula, the rest of us are at my place. G's family is meeting over here also. We need you to come tell us what you know and maybe we can get to the bottom of this, or at least help the police find out who did this to G and why." Dee placed her hand on her hip, confirming her invite.

"Yeah, no doubt. I'm on my way. Text me the address." Paula sounded like she was rushing right out the door.

"Damn, y'all. This seems like a dream. Jeremiah was all kinds of crazy for real. Shit, I thought the police were gon' let him go for a minute." Dee grabbed her heart in fear.

"Right. I was like, please God, don't let him let that man go. He gon' kill us all." Biggie joked.

"Hey, y'all." Peaches sounded serious. "What if Jeremiah was telling the truth?" She stopped for a response.

"What are you talking about?" Dee questioned.

"You said G told you she saw him following her, right? Biggie questioned.

"Yes, but she saw Big Rob too. And when that voice picked up the phone, they knew it was me. The voice said Peaches plain as day." Peaches yelled out!

What? What are you saying? You think Big Rob did this to G? No way. Big Rob didn't do this. I know he didn't," Biggie defended.

"What? He said he was gon' get her, and look what he did to me. So G didn't have shit coming. Look, I know my husband and when he says he gon' get you, you just as good as got, okay Big?. And anyway, how the hell you gon' tell me about my husband?" Peaches was offended.

Dee looked back and forth. She knew how, but this was not the time or place for that.

"I wasn't trying to tell you about your husband. I'm just saying he don't seem like the type."

"What? Why are you defending Rob?" Peaches started to feel some kind of way.

"Look, y'all, as far as we know, she saw Rob *and* Jeremiah. Both of those muthafuckas suspect. All we can do is wait and see what Paula has to add her side of what happened when her and G was together and get something concrete." Dee didn't want this situation to take away from finding out what happened to G-mama.

The family began to show up. Dee was not in the mood for it all, but she had to be hospitable. After what went down with her and G, she had better be downright graceful.

As Dee greeted everyone and served hors d'oeuvres and drinks, the doorbell rang.

"It's Paula." She announces herself.

"Hey girl." Dee gave her a big hug.

"Hey, Dee, Peaches, Biggie." Paula said as tears ran down her cheeks.

Paula stared at them and shook her head. "Damn, this is sick yo. I was just in the car with her not hours ago and to hear this shit?" She shook her head again in disbelief.

"Hey, y'all, the news is on." G's aunt yelled to everyone standing around.

"Thank you for tuning in to the ten o'clock news. I'm

Karrie Grant and I'm here on Noble Road, where a young woman, Savannah Georgia Howard, was found dead in this very alley. Spectators say they heard a gunshot and saw someone walking out of the ally, but couldn't tell if it was a woman or a man. The police have attorney Jeremiah Willard in custody as the number suspect... This just in... the police have another suspect, Robert Miller, better known as Big Rob on the street, I'm told. He has also been taken into custody. This is a horrible crime. We were out here today when some of Savannah's family were out here and their tears shook the entire crowd. Even I shed a tear for young Savannah. The police have nothing else for us as of now. But stay tuned. This is Karri Grant."

"Wow, Peaches, you really turned your husband in?" Biggie said, stunned by the news.

"Hell, yes. I don't want him thinking he can get away with this. And what is to you, Biggie? I mean, really."

"Wait, Peaches you think your man did this? And Dee, you think yo' man did it? I'm not the smartest pin in the box, but it sounds like y'all got some dirty little secret jumping off up in here." Paula sucked her teeth and rolled her neck.

"Umm hmm," G's aunt agreed. "Look my niece went through a lot as a child. She was given to me because her momma always had to have a man. And they were some no-good men that liked little girls. She had been touched and violated in ways I never heard of before. She was all over the place and we let her be her because she had been through so much. We knew it wasn't right in God's eyes, but we didn't bother her because she had already been chased out of schools and churches. Even some of our family didn't deal with her. And y'all was all she spoke about. So if y'all was close, it must be something in between the twist."

And now all the family was standing around staring.

"Look, it's simpler then y'all might think. Then again, maybe not. But once we get it all together, we'll fill everybody in on the matter at hand." Biggie drew back a breath then led Dee, Peaches, and Paula into the kitchen.

"Look, this is crazy enough with all that we know. We can't bring the family into it. They already had issues with G being bi-sexual. Do you think if they knew all that was going on, it would be any easier?" Biggie defended her actions.

"No, I guess not." Dee agreed with Biggie.

"Paula, we need to know what you know. Hopefully it can help us tie our stories together." Dee said as she poured herself some juice.

"Well, after you bitch-slapped G..." Paula began.

Dee's stomach sunk in her feet.

Paula saw the look on Dee's face and felt bad. "Sorry, but you did."

"It's cool. Go on." Dee waved her hand dismissively, hoping Paula wouldn't say it again.

Paula continued. "Well, G and I was about to go to my house so she could hook me up. But she got another phone call from an unknown number. I could hear the voice. It was like someone had one of those voice boxes. It sounded mad scary, yo."

"Yes, I heard it too, like that scary movie, umm *Scream*." Peaches cut in.

"Yea, exactly. G was scared too, I could tell."

"Did G say anything like if she knew who it was?" Biggie asked

"No, but I didn't wait around to find out. I jumped out

the car at the light," Paula said, waving her hand good-bye.

"What, why?" Biggie question.

"Why? Do you see what happened? Shit, I was scared outta my mind and I thought someone was just looking to kick her ass and it wasn't no use in both of us getting fucked up, so I bounced. G's a fighter, I'm not." Paula rolled her eyes.

Biggie and Peaches laughed. "Paula you're crazy."

"Shit, I'm for real."

But Dee didn't have laugher in her. She felt guilty. Had she not sent G packing, she just might be alive. Dee would never forgive herself.

Everyone sat around talking and drinking and crying some more. They discussed some funeral things, but no one could bear any of that tonight. Around 10:00 p.m. they said their good nights and G's family members headed home. Paula left too.

Dee called the detective and told him all the details that Paula had shared. The detective reported that they had some evidence but it still wasn't enough.

CHAPTER 20

On the day of the funeral G's family had arrived at Dee's house early. There was a big fuss about who should be riding in the family cars. Of course, everyone wanted to ride and felt they had the right to. Although Dee paid for the whole funeral, the family still felt like her, Biggie, and Peaches shouldn't ride.

It had been five days since G's murder and Dee still hadn't let go the thought of it being her fault.

As Biggie gather everyone together for prayer, and Dee tried to keep herself from vomiting, Peaches' phone began to ring.

"Hello?" Peaches answered softly.

"Peaches, put it away!" G's aunt yelled at her. "We're trying to have prayer."

"Rob, what do want?" She was shocked to hear her husband's voice.

Biggie looked up from the circle when she heard Peaches say Rob's name.

"What the fuck's going on? Y'all think I killed that bitch?" Rob was furious.

"Hell yeah, I think you did it. You said she was next and after what you did to me... I know she had nothing coming. Muthafucka, I know you. You're fucked up." Peaches began to cry.

"Bitch, if anything I should've killed yo' ass. You up dyking with a homeless ass bitch. Look, I believe the bitch got what she deserved, but I didn't kill her."

"Whatever, muthafucka." Peaches slammed the phone to the ground and watched it break into a million pieces.

G's aunts began to hum choir hymns, acting as if the cussing was going blocks their blessing.

Biggie wanted to ask if Rob was out. She really believed in heart he was innocent, but she had crossed the line too much already. If Peaches had one ounce of an idea of what went down, she would probably start a killing spree of her own.

"Let us pray." The aunt started grabbing hands.

Dee got up and reached out to Peaches who was crying. She rocked her friend slowly back and forth.

The eldest aunt began into prayer. "Father of God, we come together to release an angel from this world into the light of heaven. Father, we don't know what plans you have for us on this earth, but we know when you say it's time to come home, it's time. Savannah lived a wild life, father, a sinful life…"

"Amen!" another aunt yelled in spirit.

The praying aunt continued. "And it was matter of time before it caught up with her. I raised my sister's child in the name of Christ, praying she wouldn't grow up with lustful ways like my sister, but sometime Father of God, children go off into their own thing. But we ask you right now, Father, give us strength. Give us guidance. Heal our hearts from this horrible loss. Father, find Savannah's killer and whatever these young girls have going on, please stop them before they end up like my Savannah."

Biggie peeped at Dee and then at Peaches with her lips turned up.

The aunt continued. "Amen, Amen, and Amen."

They all got into the limos and headed to the church. When they arrived, there were people everywhere… family, friends, and clients. It was truly amazing.

"How could G ever have felt so un-loved with all these people here?" Peaches wowed over all the people waiting outside the church.

Just as Peaches was saying that, Biggie spotted a girl that looked very familiar to her. The girl smiled and walked past.

"Hey, that girl looks familiar." Biggie pointed.

"I don't know her," Dee said.

"Me either," Peaches co-signed.

"I feel like I should remember her." Biggie looked away, focusing back at the church.

The church was covered in flowers. Although G was being cremated, Dee thought giving her a home going out of this world was the least she could do, especially for the family members who didn't believe in cremation.

Everyone cried as the choir sang, "Precious Lord" and Boyz to Men's "End of the Road." The pastor said a few words, then invited friends and family up for two minutes each so share comments or say good-bye on G's behalf.

Shariff was the first person to get up. The aunts almost joined G-mama when they saw this big manly man wearing a lace front and a black two piece skirt suit with a net hat on, get up to the mic.

"I would like to give an honor to God, Pastor, and all of you here on the behalf of Ms. Savannah, who I knew as G-mama. Woo!"

Shariff began to cry. "I haven't been in a church and only you, Ms. Thang..." Shariff turned to look at G's casket. "Only you would have me up in here in six inch stilettos ruining my mascara. I love you, G-mama. Aaahh. Oh lord, I can't do this. I will always love you, G-mama. Aaahh. Oh lord, lord, lord."

Shariff's male friend walked her back to her seat. The tears sent the whole gay community that G- mama fancied, into an uproar. They were crying and screaming.

It was sad and amazing at the same time.

Next up was G-mama's cousins, followed by her favorite uncle. The uncle began, "Umm, Savannah was a mess. Hell, she got more hoes than me. Uh umm, excuse me."

The church laughed.

He continued. "Fine ones too. Sometimes we'd be hanging out and we would bet who could get more numbers between the both us. G would always win." The uncle looked up to the ceiling. "Damn, I'm gon' miss her. We were so close in age and we did everything together. I remember when G took a whipping for me. She was strong, boy, I tell you. I love you and I will miss you. Hey y'all that's my two minutes."

The uncle ended his speech like he was doing stand-up comedy.

One after another people were getting up. So many people wanted to say something about G, how she touched their lives and what not. But there were too many, so the pastor had to cut it off. The usher gathered everyone for one more view before closing the casket. It began to get crazy and emotional in there. Just as it was time for the family to walk around, Jeremiah came strolling down the aisle.

Dee couldn't believe her eyes. *The nerve of this motherfucka,* she thought to herself. *Is he crazy, or heartless?* The family and friends followed and walked around to view the body once more and left out the door.

"Biggie, did you see him?" Dee asked as they grabbed hands to walk outside.

"Who?" Biggie quickly scanned the area looking for Big Rob.

"Jeremiah. He's here." Dee whispered.

"What? Here? Where is that crazy motherfucka?" Peaches searched for him, ready to lose her mind completely.

"I don't know, but if he says anything…"

"Dee." Jeremiah bumped into her from behind, cutting her off.

Without even turning around to look at him, Dee snapped. "What the fuck are you doing here, you disrespectful bastard?"

"Dee, stop. You have to believe me. I didn't do this shit. I love you and I couldn't stand her, but…"

Dee spun around and put her hand in his face. "Don't you dare talk down against her. Get out!"

Everyone turned around and looked at Dee. She was crying and holding her stomach.

Shariff and a few people from the club G fancied were standing off to the side of them.

"I don't want to have anything to do with you." Dee peered at Jeremiah with extreme hate in her eyes.

"Dee, we have a child."

"I don't want you or this child. I don't want any part of you." Dee's chest was filled with anger as she walked closer to Jeremiah.

He suddenly grabbed Dee's arms tight.

Shariff walked up using his manly deep voice and said, "Hold on, brown sugar. Any friend of G mama's is a friend of mine and it doesn't seem like you're being friendly to my friend."

Jeremiah looked at Shariff. "Mofo, if don't get out my face I'll do yo' mama a favor and slap all the bitch outta you." Jeremiah balled his fists. He was homophobic and pissed that this faggot was stepping to him.

Just then all the beautifully dressed men walked over.

"Try it," one said.

Another said, "You and what army?"

Another took his jacket off. "Come on, cupcake. I won't even take my heels off."

"Jeremiah, this is a funeral. Leave and stay the fuck away from me. Forever." Dee tried to bring focus back to G-mama's funeral.

Jeremiah walked away, like a lost puppy. Pissed and sad at the same time, he got in his BMW and pecled off.

They loaded G casket into the limo and rode her around the city then to the funeral home where the cremation was to take place.

Everyone gathered back at the church for the repast.

The food was covering one side of the room and there were not enough tables to fit everyone so some people had to eat in the sanctuary.

"Dee, are you really gon' get rid of the baby?" Peaches asked in curiosity.

"I honestly don't know. I mean, how I can look at my child knowing his or her father murdered G?"

"Yes, but you don't know if he did it. It could have just as well been Rob."

"Either way, Jeremiah can't be trusted. I will not be married to a man with so many issues, or have him raising my child even."

Biggie started to feel emotional with this conversation, she didn't believe in abortions. She got up walked to the punch bowl. She joined in a conversation with some clients from the shop, when her phone buzzed.

Peaches was sitting close so she grabbed it for her. When Peaches looked at the number, she couldn't believe her eyes. "What the fuck?" It was Big Rob's number.

Peaches burned a hole in Biggie's back.

"What, girl?" Dee grabbed Peaches mouth.

Peaches was on fire. "Nothing!" She knew there had been enough drama at G's funeral and she wouldn't dare give G's aunts more to look down on them for. But she almost couldn't hold it.

Peaches read the text with Rob's voice in mind. *"Hi sexy, I'm out. I hope you didn't think I would do that shit, I mean I hate that bitch but after being with you, I wasn't on it no more. I know y'all was close though, so I'm here if you want to talk or need a shoulder to cry on, or just need me to hold you."*

Biggie lifted her cup to Peaches to ask if she wanted punch. Peaches tilted her head and rolled her eyes at the same time, keeping face. All along thinking what a back-stabbing bitch Biggie was and she was going pay for it soon enough.

CHAPTER 21

After the repast, Shariff told everyone to meet at the club for a home going after party, Dee and Biggie thought that was too inappropriate and declined. Peaches was on one and was too involved in her thoughts to even think about it. So they retired and got dropped off at Dee's.

First Peaches walked in, then Dee. As soon as Biggie closed the door behind them, Wham! Peaches hit her hard as fuck in the face.

"What the fuck?" Biggie grabbed her bleeding face.

Peaches drew her fist back again. Wham! "I'll kill you. Bitch, you fucking my husband?"

She beat Biggie until there was no more room for bruises. Biggie never fought back. She knew she was wrong and she was caught doing just what she had judged Peaches for. Well, it wasn't exactly the same, but close enough.

Dee dropped to the floor and cried out for someone to take off whatever curse had been laid upon them. She always knew there was other powers than God out there, but never knew they could touch her and her surroundings.

She screamed, "God, please take it away. I pray to you. I don't know what I've done, but I pray you take this evil out of our lives. Make it the way it was. Lord, do Your will!"

Peaches beat Biggie unconscious. With Biggie's blood all over her, she walked upstairs into the bathroom and sat in the tub, fully dressed, no water or anything, and cried her eyes out.

Dee thought Biggie was dead. She didn't say a word.

She crawled over to her lifeless friend, laid her on her lap and rocked her back and forth. She rocked for hours before Jeremiah came in, saw her, and called for an ambulance.

Dee was relieved to see him, and afraid at the same time. He knew she was in shock, so he didn't mention the drama, the baby or anything. When the ambulance arrived he let Dee ride with Biggie, who was still alive, and he followed behind them. As she sat in the ambulance, hearing the siren and staring at Biggie's horribly bruised face she realized that everything that glittered wasn't gold and that there are many uglies in the beauty salon...

DAYS LATER...

Biggie stayed unconscious for days. She dreamt of G-mama over and over again. The funeral, the murder site. She wondered why in her dream this image kept appearing. She needed to know who this familiar, but unfamiliar person was. A smile, from the shop to the alley to the funeral. Over and over. Who was this?

Suddenly her heart monitor started to beep like crazy. Biggie jumped out of her unconscious state. Her eyes widened. She was somewhat dizzy, but said, "I KNOW WHO DID IT!"

DISCUSSION QUESTIONS:

1. Do you think G-mama's childhood had an effect on her bi-sexuality? Explain.
2. Why do you think Biggie had a box full of guns at home?
3. Do you think Jeremiah really loves Dee or is he just about the baby?
4. Do you have any friends like Peaches who might not jump in or have your back in a physical altercation?
5. What did you think of Big Rob? Was he justified in how he reacted when he discovered Peaches' secret?
6. Have you ever had a stalker or got involved with someone who became a fatal attraction?
7. Who is your favorite character and why?
8. Do you have "Uglies" or crazy drama at the beauty salon you go to? Or have you heard about any shop drama?
9. What do you think is going to happen in "Uglies of the Beauty Salon 2: Still Ugly"?

ABOUT THE AUTHOR

Ms. BBC brings creativity to everything she does. She's an Intimacy consultant of her own company Body2body Intimacy, singer, reggae promoter, an entrepreneur and an author. She believes strongly in empowering all women, however her main focus reaches out upon plus-size women. In fact, her moniker, BBC, stands for Big Body Chick. She encourages women to be healthy and love the skin they're in. *Uglies of the Beauty Salon* is her debut novel.